THE SEER CHRONICLES

VOLUME 1

DEB LOGAN

COPYRIGHT

PRAISE FOR DEB LOGAN

Praise for *Faery Unexpected*

Old Ozark Gal from Amazon: Five stars: "This is a well-written, entertaining read geared for young adults, but fun for all ages. Pick up your copy today!"

———

Diane from Amazon: Five stars: "I enjoyed reading it. Love the characters that have been created. It is one to add to your TBR list."

———

Reader from Amazon: Five stars: "...a fun interesting read. Kept my attention."

———

Michelle from Amazon: Four stars: "This was a fun read ... Very imaginative, going to share this ebook with my teenage niece, she will love it!"

———

Praise for *Thunderbird*

Reader from Amazon: Five stars: "This has been a great story and experience for me! It hits just about every single check in my list. Including the all important "will I re-read it!" (I will!) I look forward to reading more titles by this author. And it would be a great story to read aloud to children. Thanks Ms Logan!"

———

Josephine from Amazon: Four stars: "Filled with magical adventure and learning. Told in a Native American Indian folktale kind of way. It was not what I expected but I enjoyed it just the same. It did keep me reading. I would definitely recommend!"

———

Reader from Amazon: Four stars: "This was a great adventure and a great read. Good vs evil. Learning Trust. Learning about the magic within and that of the universe!"

———

DeAnna from Amazon: Four stars: "...Fast action, not a lot of blah blah blah, good characters, interesting plot and locations: this book receives my kid-brain seal of approval."

———

Praise for *Cinnamon Chou*

Cece from Amazon: Five stars: "Deb Logan does a great job of telling an exciting story for a younger audience. I recommend it to newer readers. Really nice cover artwork, too!"

INTRODUCTION

When I first imagined Artie and Jed I had no idea where their story would take me. Their unusual partnership began on a fall day in a neighborhood park in Colorado, but I never dreamed their association would take them to Ireland (To Have...and To Hold) and later to Scotland (Paladin Shield). I also had no idea where their special abilities came from or that they were part of a long line of *Seers*!

I've enjoyed my journey with these two special young people, and I hope you will too.

Thank you for reading!

—Deb

TERRORS

CHAPTER 1

A terror approached.

I cast my eyes down, fixing my gaze on the worn institutional tile beneath my feet, counting my heartbeats until it would be safe to look up again. The count was ingrained. A long practiced skill that no longer required my attention. Instead, my mind wandered, wondering what it would be like to unknow these denizens of the unseen world? To be a normal teen, with normal perceptions; a girl who walked this earth with no realization of what stalked her every step?

Unfortunately, that was not my life.

The count ended. I raised my eyes and glanced around quickly to reorient myself. High-ceilinged hallway, walls lined with lockers and classroom doors. Students milled around, chatted with friends, complained about their schedules. Everyone studiously avoided noticing me.

Yep. Same old invisible girl. The building might have changed, but the experience remained the same. I stepped away from the wall, pushed into the throng, and made my way to class without making eye contact with any of my peers.

I'd hoped high school would be different from middle

school, that somehow, miraculously, the halls of McKinley High would be full of kids anxious to be my friends, and gloriously free of the beings that haunted my waking nightmares.

I'd been stupid of course. No such place existed.

Every single person I'd ever met considered me a freak. If truth be told, that even included my parents. And the others? The terrors? They ruled our world from the shadows, influencing our thoughts with whispered commands that were no more noticeable than the sigh of mosquito wings. Veiled suggestions of disease and despair, murmurs of treachery and disloyalty. Human souls rotted at the whim of foul creatures who fed from our life-force and lapped up our baser emotions like ice cream. No one knew of their existence, so no one guarded against their intrusions.

No one but me — and I'd learned early to hide my knowledge.

Mom and Dad had worried when my imaginary friends terrified me instead of entertaining. Other kids feared the boogieman in the closet or the monster under the bed, but were easily appeased by a nightlight or an extra bedtime story. Not me. Never me. I knew my monsters personally, recognized their reality with a sharp twist of terror in my gut.

Other kids embraced pacification, accepted that the monsters they perceived lived only in their imaginations. Not me. I learned to close my eyes, duck my head, and count the beats of my heart until the unholy creatures tired of watching me and moved on.

My parents noted my odd moments of seeming paralysis and sought psychological counseling. I developed yet another necessary life skill: I learned to lie. The doctor couldn't explain away my certain knowledge of monsters, but I could explain away my parents' concerns. Eventually, the adults in my life were appeased and I continued my uneasy existence, camouflaging myself from both my parents' concern and the notice of the creatures that stalk humanity.

I wished I understood why I could see my terrors and others couldn't. Why was I singled out to endure this curse? More than anything, I longed for a companion in this surreal world, someone to share my fears and woes ... but then, would I truly wish this ungodly knowledge on another human being? Especially a person I might learn to consider a friend? I don't know. Misery — at least mine, really would love some company.

And so I embarked on my first day of high school. Doomed to another four years of harassment at the hands of classmates who had no clue about the creatures that stalked them. Four more years of jokes about space cadets, morons, and total dweeb losers from kids who might have been my friends if only ... if only I could unknow the unseen, or my peers could have their blind eyes opened. Neither of which was going to happen.

I rolled my sturdy red and black backpack off my shoulders, claimed a seat at the back of my first class, and tried not to focus on the creature hovering just behind the teacher's left shoulder. Not an easy task; to give my attention to the solid little woman in her gray tweed skirt, pristine white blouse, and charcoal-gray cardigan, while pretending not to see the elongated, ethereal creature shrouded in a cloak that might have been made of wisps of fog. The real-as-the-desk-under-my-fingers entity with blue-tinged skin and flat black eyes who stood right behind the oblivious woman.

The noxious, evil creature that breathed terror into every day of my life bent nearly double to whisper instructions in my teacher's perfectly mundane ear. The contrast between the bright, cheerful red pepper earrings dangling from her earlobe and the scabrous three-fingered hand stroking her neck made me want to puke.

I shook my head, sucked in a deep breath, and reminded

myself that giving them mind-space wasn't wise. The secret to anonymity was to control my reactions, to give no sign that I noticed when the creature moved or spoke. I'd become adept through years of practice, but only when I remained calm and uninvolved.

Controlling a shudder, I tightened my focus on my teacher as she read our morning's schedule. I couldn't afford to think about the slimy feel of their fingers as they stroked my cheek, or remember the horrible sibilant hiss of their voices as they whispered 'suggestions' in my ear. Giving brain-space to such thoughts made it so much harder to pretend they weren't there, to imagine that this was just another school day and I was just another terror-blind student.

I closed my eyes for an instant mimicking boredom, but giving myself a moment's rest from the stress of acting. If they gave out Academy Awards for avoiding terror detection, I'd be a shoo-in.

That's when it happened. The atmosphere in the class changed, became charged, and my eyes flew open. I skimmed the room looking for trouble — and found it immediately. A classmate, a boy I'd never seen before, stood paralyzed at the front of the class staring directly into the terror's dark gaze.

He looked so normal. White tee-shirt covered with an untucked blue plaid shirt; acid-washed jeans, the knees going white and nearly threadbare; scuffed black sneakers. His hair was dark and shaggy, with ragged bangs half-concealing his eyes. But those eyes weren't focused on the normal world. He was definitely studying the terror poised behind our teacher.

He inhaled deeply, pointed a trembling finger at the creature, licked his lips, and said in a shaky, yet fierce voice, "Begone, demon! I command you in the name of Michael the Hunter; leave this place and never return."

I sucked in a breath and barely kept myself from screaming a warning. Did he know what he risked? Calling its attention to his awareness? I bit my lip until I tasted blood, held my breath, and waited for his doom.

The rest of the class, teacher included, stared at him, mouths agape, and then titters of nervous giggles flared, but he took no notice. He stood his ground as the terror rushed him, stumbling back a step as the monster flowed through him and into oblivion.

The class erupted in hoots and catcalls while the teacher banged on her desk for order.

I breathed a sigh of relief as my heart rate regulated.

And then it happened.

The boy turned, pale as ice, and caught my gaze. Me. The only other person in the room who wasn't laughing, who probably looked even more drained and terrified than he did. He shrugged, nodded in acknowledgement, and turned to face his sentence: a trip to the principal's office for daring to come to school under the influence.

CHAPTER 2

I didn't see the guy again until lunch. I'd managed to keep my head down through my morning classes and had navigated the cafeteria crowd out into the late fall sunshine of the enclosed terrace. Other kids, popular kids, even not-so-popular-but-we-have-friends kids, sat around picnic tables in chattering clusters. I knew better than to join any of them. If I did, all talk would cease and an uneasy silence would descend until one-by-one the others drifted away to more congenial tables.

At least no one threw food at me anymore.

I shambled across the terrace, avoiding everyone, human and terror alike, until I came to a low retaining wall separating the flagstone patio from the landscaping. Huddled beneath a stunted aspen tree, I perched on the wall, unwrapped my sandwich and took a bite. The bread was a little soggy, but a burst of tart mustard shocked my taste buds and woke my appetite. I'd just stuffed the last bit of crust into my mouth and was reaching for my water bottle when a shadow fell across my space and two sneaker-clad feet entered my field of vision.

Glancing up, I shaded my eyes and found the new guy standing in front of me, tray in hand.

"Mind if I join you?"

I shrugged and swallowed, my throat suddenly tight. "Sure. Why not?"

"I saw you in first block," he said, settling beside me and dropping his tray on the grass beside a few scraggly primroses.

"Yeah. Well, I couldn't help but notice you." My gaze slid to his face, but skittered away before he could make eye contact. "First day at McKinley High?"

His turn to shrug. He tilted his head back and took a long swig of water. I watched the play of muscles in his neck as he swallowed, fascinated by the way his Adam's apple bobbed.

"My family just moved here. Hadn't planned on making an entrance, but, well, you know, shit happens."

I lowered my eyes again before he could catch me looking, and nodded. "Yeah. I know."

"You saw what happened, didn't you?"

Surprise knocked me into his trap. My eyes widened and I found myself staring right into his gray-eyed gaze. My pulse raced and heat suffused my face. "Well, sure. Everyone did."

He shook his head without releasing my gaze. "No they didn't, but you did. You saw it all. You saw the creature I banished."

Sweat beaded my upper lip and froze there. I didn't talk about the terrors. Not to anyone. My heart thudded harder than a bass drum and then slowed to a minimal blip. Darkness edged my vision as blood retreated to my core, leaving me dizzy and a little slow.

This wouldn't do! I needed my wits about me, clear and sharp. This guy was speaking openly about the creatures I'd been hiding from my entire life. Every cell in my being screamed, "Danger!"

I gulped a huge breath, grabbed my half empty water bottle

and squeezed it like my life depended on holding tight. I don't know. Maybe it did. I wrenched my gaze from his steady gray eyes and leaned forward so that my long dark hair screened my face.

Fear screamed at me to jump and run. I should. I knew I should. He'd seen through my defenses, and my survival depended on staying invisible. I needed to get as far away from him as I could...

...but I didn't. I just sat there squeezing my water bottle and breathing like I'd run a marathon.

He sighed. Sadness embodied. Disappointment made audible.

I peeked past my hair. He stared across the terrace; an expression of melancholy loneliness etched his face. I knew that look. I wore it often myself.

Twisting off the cap of my poor, battered water bottle, I took a sip and whispered, "What's your name?"

He cocked his head and caught my gaze, a sparkle of hope lighting his eyes. "Jed Kendrick. What's yours?"

"Artie Woodward."

A slow smile curled the edges of his lips. "Nice to meet you, Artie Woodward. I've only known one other seer. What about you?"

He'd known someone else like us? Questions crowded my brain, but I just shook my head. I wanted to trust him, but it was too soon for confidences.

"Don't talk much, do you." It wasn't a question, but a statement of fact.

"No. Quiet is safer."

He nodded. "Understood. How many shrinks have they dragged you to?"

A defiant smile tipped my own lips and I sat a little straighter. "Only one. I'm a quick study."

His eyes widened and he laughed. The sound bubbled up from deep within and spilled past his lips. It winged around us, weaving a circle of camaraderie in its wake. When the outburst passed, he wiped moisture from his eyes and grinned at me. "Think you can teach me that trick? I've seen at least six shrinks and been institutionalized twice. Not that it's done anybody any good."

I reached out and touched his arm, an unprecedented familiarity. "I'm so sorry, Jed." The words were no sooner out than a terror glided toward us, undoubtedly attracted by Jed's laughter. I shrank back, pulled my hair down around my face, stared at the ground and thought invisible thoughts.

After the requisite number of heartbeats, I glanced up to find Jed staring at me. But the terror had moved on without stopping.

"How did you do that?"

I frowned, my heart still thundering from the near miss. "Do what?"

"It didn't see us. It moved right on past as if we weren't even here." He shook his head, eyes narrowed in concentration. "We need to talk, Artie. Compare notes."

My pulse spiked. I'd never had a friend. Never had anyone look at me with the mixture of awe and respect Jed was giving me. I straightened, pushed my hair behind my ears and smiled. Okay, it wasn't much of a smile, but then my smile muscles were highly under-developed.

"I'd like that."

CHAPTER 3

*T*he rest of the day passed in a fog of contentment. I'd call it happiness, only I'd never really been happy before, so I wasn't sure what that felt like. But I was definitely more at ease, more content to be me, than I had ever been. The other kids in my classes even seemed kinder. No one spoke to me or smiled at me or gave any indication of being aware of my presence, but neither did they call me names, bump books out of my arms, or do any of the other myriad little annoyances that normally made my school days hell. All in all, it was an auspicious start to the school year.

I should have known it couldn't last.

The late afternoon sun blinded me as I stepped through the side door that led to the parking area where my bus would be waiting. Against my long-ingrained habit, my hair was tucked behind my ears and my posture erect. My day had given me a false sense of security, and I walked with a little bounce in my step. The air smelled of fresh cut grass, hot pavement, and car exhaust. White puffy clouds floated overhead, pushed along by a light, refreshing breeze. In short, it was a beautiful fall day and I gloried in it.

"Hey, freak!" A male voice called, yanking me from my pleasant reverie. "Where do you think you're going?"

I whirled, knowing the guy meant me. After all, I'd been the resident freak for as long as I could remember, but I was wrong. Someone else had stolen my limelight. Jed stood in a rough circle of athletic-looking boys. I hadn't paid much attention to his physique earlier, but he looked tall, gangly and under-fed compared to the jocks surrounding him.

As I stood rooted to the sidewalk, one of the boys pushed Jed, while another pulled his backpack from his arms and tossed it away.

"Who do you think you are, screw-up?" The speaker swaggered forward, ruffled Jed's hair before shoving him backward.

Jed stumbled and fell against two of the other guys, who pushed him back toward their leader.

The guy strutted around Jed, measuring his lack of reaction. "What's wrong, freak? No girls around to impress? I think you need a lesson in how things are done around here." He turned to his comrades. "What do you think? Should we teach this freak some manners?"

The other guys laughed, a dark growling sound, and shouted their agreement.

Things were about to get uglier than they knew. Several terrors drifted in their direction. My heart skipped a beat. I glanced at the bus; my escape route was filling up. The driver would close the doors and leave soon. But Jed was in trouble. My only friend in the world needed help. But what could I do? I mean, until his arrival, I'd been the butt of all the jokes. The one bullied by guys like those surrounding Jed. I had no power. No way to protect him.

Besides, I barely knew him.

And as for the terrors, he'd banished one this morning — something I'd never managed. He could do it again. Of course, that was assuming the jocks didn't beat him to a pulp for mouthing off while they were taunting him.

I chewed my lip, indecision eating at my gut. I had to choose. Now. The moment would pass and my chance would be lost forever. Which would it be? Safety, or the possibility of a friend?

No contest. I'd never had a friend before.

With a quick wave to the bus driver, I ran toward the group of guys, snagged Jed's backpack, and elbowed my way to his side. Grabbing his arm, I thrust the pack against his chest where he clutched it by instinct, then prodded him toward the bus.

"What are you doing? Our bus is leaving! You can mess around with your friends tomorrow. Right now we have to get home. Mom is waiting."

Surprise and inane chatter worked in my favor. The bullies fell back for a second, glancing at each other. I took advantage of their confusion to propel Jed to the bus. We leapt up the steps and inside, just as the driver closed the doors.

"Take a seat, you two," he said, shaking his head. "And be on time tomorrow."

I ducked my head, shielding myself from his view with my hair and mumbled, "Yes, sir." Then dragged Jed to the back of the bus where we settled in the very last row.

"Thanks," he whispered. He dropped his backpack between his feet and stared out the window at the gang of guys who were still watching the bus, shaking their heads. He ran his hands through his hair and slotted a sideways glance in my direction. "Do you have any idea where this bus is going?"

I tucked my hair behind my ears and grinned. "Yep. It'll drop us off about three blocks from my house. You got a problem with that?"

A wicked smile curved his mouth and lit his eyes. "Nope. I've never been rescued by a girl and then whisked away to her house before." He winked at me. "Kinda cool, ya know?"

I giggled and reached to tug my hair across my heated face, but Jed caught my fingers.

"Don't," he said quietly. "You don't need to hide from me." He pulled my hand to his lips and gazed into my eyes as he kissed my knuckles.

Shock widened my eyes while my heart pounded so loud I was surprised he didn't hear it. Totally speechless, I just sat there staring into his gray eyes.

He smirked, released my hand and held out his own. "Friends?"

My knuckles still tingling from the warmth of his lips, I placed my hand in his and shook. "Friends."

He relaxed and stared out the window for a few seconds, then glanced back at me. "Back there," he said, jerking his chin to indicate the direction of the school, "I didn't know you could string that many words together. What came over you?"

My cheeks flushed again, but I resisted the urge to duck behind my hair and shrugged instead. "Dunno. Looked like you were in trouble, and, well … they were just guys."

To anyone else, that statement would've sounded stupid, maybe even moronic, but Jed understood. He nodded. "Yeah. I know. I wouldn't have enjoyed getting beat up, but they weren't …well, you know."

I nodded. I did. We definitely needed to talk, but this wasn't the place. We were unguarded, exposed. I rarely spoke of the terrors — who would listen? — but I certainly didn't talk about them on a public school bus surrounded by dozens of kids who were clueless to their danger.

We settled into a companionable silence while the bus rumbled on, stopping every few blocks to disgorge students. Finally, when there were less than a dozen of us still seated, the big yellow vehicle rolled to a halt at my designated stop. I nudged Jed, stood, and shuffled down the narrow aisle following two other kids. When we hit the pavement, the other two waved to their friends who still sat on the bus and wandered off to the right. I pulled Jed left.

"Alone at last," he quipped as the bus pulled away from the corner.

I rolled my eyes. "Cute."

"Nice! She thinks I'm cute."

My face flamed again, but I couldn't help smiling. Jed had that effect on me.

"You're weird," I said after a few steps along the shaded sidewalk. We strolled through a quiet residential neighborhood. Freshly mown lawns, neatly tended flower beds with the last remaining blooms of summer nodding in a gentle breeze, tall trees lined the street guarding the sidewalk from the late afternoon sun. All in all, a pleasant day … especially since there wasn't a terror in sight. I breathed a sigh of relief and quirked a glance at Jed. "How come you're so friendly and, well, happy? Sounds like you've had it even tougher than me."

"Cool. She thinks I'm cute AND friendly." He rubbed his hands together and grinned. "This is going better than expected!"

I couldn't help it, my eyes rolled again and a groan escaped my lips. He really was too much.

His expression grew serious and the light left his eyes. A fierce determination hardened his face. "I act happy and friendly because how I feel is my choice. I refuse to let them control me, control my life." The ferocity faded and he smiled a little sadly. "I can't change what I see, but I can choose how I react. Just like you obviously chose what to say to the shrink to reassure your parents."

I nodded. "We can teach each other a lot."

"That's my game plan," he said, another grin lighting his

features. "Plus, it's nice to finally have someone who understands."

"Tell me about it. Seeing them makes you lonely."

"Yeah. You can't talk about them or you end up in the loony bin."

"But it's hard to talk about normal stuff, 'cause it all seems so trivial and unimportant compared to, well, them."

He nodded. "That about sums it up."

We turned a corner and I pointed ahead. "That's my house. The yellow one with the white picket fence."

He stopped dead in his tracks, stared at my house, glanced sideways at me, and then laughed out loud. Laughed so hard he had to shuffle a few steps to lean against a maple tree while he caught his breath.

"What?" I asked, annoyance creeping into the word.

"I might have known," he said, wiping his eyes on the sleeve of his sweatshirt. "I meet the most un-normal girl in the world and she lives in a totally stereotypical suburban house, complete with white picket fence." He waved at the neighborhood in general and my house in particular. "I mean, really? Can you get any more Apple-Pie-American than this?"

I stared around me, absorbing the landscape, drinking down the scene I'd experienced every day of my life — and saw it with new eyes. Jed was right. This street, this neighborhood, my home; each was so normal, so stereotypically American upper-middle-class, and yet here I stood, as totally and completely *not* normal as it was possible to imagine. No wonder I'd never truly belonged here. A slow smile tugged at my lips. I hadn't realized how badly I'd needed someone like Jed in my life. Someone who could challenge my perceptions, make me take stock of my blind acceptance of other people's norm. Other people's. Never mine. Maybe Jed and I could define our own version of normality.

Slipping my hand into the crook of his arm, I drew him

toward my house. "Come on. We've got things to discuss, notes to compare, and plans to make."

He grinned and performed a courtly bow. "Your wish is my command, milady."

CHAPTER 4

*M*om met us at the front door. She tried to hide the look of shocked amazement that widened her eyes, rounded her mouth, and made her look even younger than me, but failed miserably. She was so surprised to see me with a boy at my side that she actually stammered.

Well. Really. Who could blame her? I'd never, ever brought a friend home. Not once.

"Er ... uhm ... I-I'm Estelle, Artie's mother," she finally managed to blurt, holding the screen door open, but blocking entry with her body.

"It's okay, Mom," I said, taking the door from her and nudging her to one side. No go. She was firmly planted and totally oblivious. I sighed. "This is Jed. He knows I don't have any friends, so you can relax."

Jed smiled his charming smile and stuck out his hand. "A pleasure to meet you, Mrs. Woodward. Artie and I met at school. My family just moved here, so she's showing me around."

"Er ... uhm ...N-nice to meet you, Jed." Mom gave me a side-long look, but her color was returning to normal.

"Mom. Chill. Is it okay if we come inside?"

Finally the penny dropped. Mom's cheeks reddened and she backed away from the door into the front hall. "Of course! How silly of me. Standing here blocking the door. Come right in, Jed. What did you say your last name was?"

Jed stepped inside and I slipped past Mom to drop my backpack on a chair in the living room.

"Kendrick, Jed Kendrick. My folks just moved here from upstate New York. Dad's the new pastor at the Evangelical church."

I froze where I stood, jaw hanging open in shock. My new friend, the only other person I'd ever known who could see the terrors was a preacher's kid? I forced my mouth closed and stared into those guileless gray eyes. Made sense in a way. Who else would have the authority to command the unholy?

"Well, how nice." Mom gave me a sidelong look, but her color was returning to normal. "I'll look forward to meeting your parents. Are you and Artie in the same grade?"

"Yes, ma'am," he said. "We met in first period and then found each other again at lunch time."

Okay. Enough chit-chat with the parental unit. Time to get down to work.

"I'm going to show Jed the park, Mom," I said, grabbing Jed's sleeve and dragging him down the hall toward the back door. "Would you mind driving him home before dinner? He got on the wrong bus by mistake."

"Of course. I'll be happy to drive you home. Do you need to call your parents and let them know where you are?"

He planted his feet to stop me from dragging him further from Mom and pulled a cell phone from his back pocket. "Already taken care of," he said with a grin. "If it's inconvenient for you, I'm sure Mom could use a break from unpacking, though it might take her a while to figure out how to get here."

Mom laughed. "It's no bother. Let's not add to your mother's stress. You two enjoy your walk to the park. I'll drive Jed home whenever he's ready."

I jerked my head toward the back of the house with a meaningful glance at Jed and waved over my shoulder to Mom. "See you later."

Jed followed me through the kitchen. I paused long enough to grab two apples and a couple of bottles of water from the fridge before leading him out the back door, across a brick patio, over the well-manicured back lawn, and through a thin spot in the evergreen hedge that bounded the rear of our yard. We emerged in an empty lot on the next street over.

"Come on," I said. "The park is just down this block."

Jed brushed a twig from his sleeve and gave me a quizzical look. "Why are we going to a park?"

I squinted both directions down the street and sprinted across to the sidewalk on the other side. "Best place I've found to think. I sit on the little kids' merry-go-round and spin slowly. Not fast enough to make me dizzy, but enough that I can keep a watch in all directions. They can't just appear out of the ground, so I have plenty of warning if one is coming."

I tossed him a bottle of water and an apple and then took a bite of my own. The flavor burst on my tongue, sweet and tart at the same time. Just the way I liked. I chewed and swallowed, twisted off the cap and took a swig of water, and then shrugged. "I figure what we need to discuss, we don't want overheard ... by anyone. The merry-go-round will give us plenty of privacy."

He nodded, following my example with the fruit, though I've got to say, the guy took huge bites. Looked like half the apple disappeared in his first mouthful. Once he'd tossed what little was left of the core, he continued the conversation as though we hadn't just taken a snack break. "Good thinking. Doors and walls might protect us from human ears, but you never know when one of them is going to glide right through brick or wood."

"I know," I agreed. "It's like the laws of physics don't apply. But I've never seen one rise out of the ground, have you?"

He considered that for a moment, took another swig of water, and said, "Nope. Can't say I have. Your merry-go-round sounds like as safe a place for a talk as we're likely to find."

I nodded and turned into a fenced walkway between houses, tugging Jed's sleeve to steer him along. We had a lot to discuss, important stuff, and I wouldn't feel at ease until we made it to the merry-go-round.

CHAPTER 5

*W*e emerged in a small, rectangular, neighborhood park, bounded on all sides by houses, with two narrow walkways leading in and one street that dead-ended into a short side. The majority of the land was flat and grassy, perfect for a game of Frisbee or tossing a ball around. Play equipment nestled at the end nearest the street access, and a tall stand of pines shaded an area of picnic tables. Jed and I walked side-by-side to the merry-go-round. The park was deserted except for the two of us.

Frankly, it didn't see much use during the week. Even after school, most of the kids were still at day-care, waiting for their parents to evacuate their cubicle jungles and pick them up for the evening. I was luckier than most. Dad worked in the next city over — he was an architect and the prestigious firm that paid our bills required a better address than our little cow-town could provide, but Mom was self-employed and worked from home. So I'd never had to do the day-care thing.

Of course, Mom's career choice may have been influenced by the decidedly weird daughter she and Dad had spawned. I shuddered and veered away from that thought.

Jed and I settled on the circular piece of play equipment. We leaned against the handrails facing each other. What I couldn't see at any given moment, Jed could. Each of us dangled one foot over the edge, giving a gentle push every now and then to keep the thing gliding squeakily on its axis.

"So," Jed said, "where do you want to begin?"

I shrugged and traced the raised pattern of the steel under my fingers. "Dunno. Never really talked about them before."

"I hear ya. Let's start at the beginning. How long have you been seeing them?"

My head snapped up and I met his gray-eyed gaze with wide eyes. "Seriously? Can you remember a time when you couldn't see them?" He just stared at me, waiting for me to answer the question. I sighed and studied the lay of the land over his shoulder. "I've always seen them. At least, I think I have. I mean, who remembers what they saw as a baby?" Satisfied that the park remained empty, I met his gaze again. "What about you?"

"I started seeing them when I was eight. I remember, because it was right after my twin brother died."

A chill ran icy fingers down my back and I shivered involuntarily.

"Oh, wow. You had a twin. I'm so sorry." I wanted to ask what happened to his brother, but bit back the question. *Don't push.*

"Yeah. I thought the first one was Jerry's ghost, but even though he was a little ... odd, he was never mean. He'd never have wanted to scare me out of my wits."

I nodded, but kept still, hoping he'd tell me more.

"That first sighting added to Jerry's death sent me straight to a shrink. I'm sure you know what that's like." He shook his head, gulped some water, and looked at me slant-wise. "Now that I'm older and have had lots of time to think about it, I think Jerry was like you. I think he could see them from birth. I'm pretty sure he spent a lot of his short life protecting me and Mom and Dad."

He propped the nearly empty water bottle in the crook of his knee and stared at his hands, flexing his fingers as though getting ready to play a piano recital. I didn't say a word. I'd already done more talking today than I usually did in a month, but more importantly, I could feel Jed's stress. He was testing the ether; testing the bond between us, deciding how much weight it would hold. Deciding if I was trustworthy enough to hear what he hadn't said yet. What he still needed to say.

Silence stretched between us. I stared over his shoulder, remaining vigilant while he made his choices. A deep sigh pulled my attention back to his face. He continued to stare at his hands, splayed now against the faded blue of well-worn jeans.

"I was with him when he died," he said, his voice so quiet I strained to hear him over the slight squeaking of the merry-go-round. "We'd been playing in the backyard when he had one of his funny spells. He went all rigid, ducking his head and muttering a string of unintelligible words while he pushed me to the ground and held me there. He had one hand over my mouth and nose. I couldn't breathe, but I knew Jerry wouldn't hurt me, so I went completely limp and held my breath, waiting for his fit to pass. Only it didn't.

"Oh, he released me, but while I caught my breath, something picked him up and tossed him aside like a rag doll. He landed hard against a tree, cracked his skull. That's what did it. That's what killed him.

"I ran to him, right through something so cold it made my fingers cramp and my lungs seize, but I didn't care. I had to get to Jerry. I was screaming like a banshee and Mom and Dad came running to see what was wrong. Dad froze, staring at us like he'd seen a ghost, but Mom ran for the phone and called 9-1-1. It didn't matter. They were too late. Everyone was too late."

He fisted his hands and looked up into my eyes. Grief and anger and terror blazed in that gaze.

"I got to him first. I grabbed his hand and shouted his name over and over again. He opened his eyes once, squeezed my fingers, and said, 'You'll have to protect them now. You can do it. Michael will help.' And then he died. Just like that, my twin was gone. My best friend. My womb-mate. The person I loved more than any other left me crying in the backyard under a maple tree."

His eyes misted with tears, and he swiped them away with short, choppy strokes. "But that wasn't all. As he breathed his last, something happened. Something transferred from Jerry to me. I don't know if I inhaled it, or it passed skin-to-skin through our clasped hands, but suddenly I could see it. Could see the creature that had killed my brother, and something more. I saw Michael. The archangel. The hunter. The destroyer of those monsters.

"But just like everyone else that afternoon, Michael was too late to save Jerry. Was almost too late to save me. When I started yelling about angels and demons, Dad snapped out of it and grabbed me. I think he thought he'd lost both his sons."

"What about the terror?" I whispered.

He sighed, a weary, this-world-is-too-heavy-for-me exhalation. "I don't know. Dad was sobbing and praying and clutching me like he'd never let go. When I finally wriggled loose and looked around, the thing had vanished."

I leaned forward and caught his hand, noting the cool slickness of the not-quite-tears on his fingers. "Thank you for telling me," I said. "You're not alone anymore. Neither of us is. I can't replace Jerry." I swallowed a lump that threatened to cut off my words, and sucked in a deep breath. "Wouldn't want to if I could. But between us, we can figure this out."

He looked up from our clasped hands and frowned. "Figure what out?"

"This. Us. There's got to be a reason we can see them. Must be something we're supposed to do with our abilities." I scrambled off the merry-go-round and paced back and forth. "I've thought about this for a while now, but with no one to talk to, no one to bounce ideas off of, I've been stuck. Why me? Why can I see them when no one else can? What's the purpose? Did God just wake up one morning and think, 'Gee, I think I'll torture Artie. Make everyone think she's paranoid and delusional. It'll be a great laugh!'

"I don't think so. I think I'm supposed to fight them, but I haven't known how."

I stopped pacing, planted my hands on my hips and gave him a daring look. "But I'm not alone anymore." I nodded to him, purpose blazing in my heart. "Today I found a teammate."

He sat still as stone for another moment, staring deep into my eyes. Then he unfolded from the play equipment and held out his hand. "Woodward and Kendrick," he said when I placed my palm against his. "Partners."

We shook on it, and then sat down side by side.

"You're right. There's more to this than God torturing teens. I'll ask Michael about it."

I slanted him a look. "So who is this Michael guy? Is he really an archangel?"

Jed shrugged. "Couldn't prove it by me. I've only seen him the once with waking eyes. Most of the time, he visits my dreams and explains stuff to me."

"Uh-huh."

He laid back, his head toward the center of the circular play disc, feet planted firmly on the ground. "Hey, he's no weirder than any of the other stuff we see, and he's actually helped me. Whatever he is, he's definitely not one of them."

I nodded, my thoughts racing. "Cool. So this partnership

may have divine assistance. I can live with that." I turned my next words over in my brain, examining them carefully before releasing them into the world. "Maybe his existence even proves my theory. I mean, if we're supposed to fight monsters, isn't it reasonable that God would provide a guide? A teacher of some kind? Otherwise, we'd end up like your brother — dead before we could even get started."

Jed covered his eyes with his forearm, but remained silent. I replayed my last words in my head and wanted to smack myself.

"I'm sorry, Jed," I whispered. "That was an incredibly insensitive thing to say." I shoved the ground with my foot, giving the merry-go-round another spurt of movement, and surveyed the perimeter. Anything was better than looking at the new friend I'd probably just alienated.

Jed sat up, his action adding to our momentum, and placed a finger on my cheek, turning my face in his direction. "Don't apologize for being right. Jerry didn't stand a chance. He was too young to take an active role. Michael shouldn't have let him; should have taught him to hide until he was older and stronger."

He dropped his hands and jumped to the ground. "Hell. I don't know, maybe he did. Maybe Jerry wouldn't listen. Maybe Jerry didn't have the knack for hiding. Whatever. He's gone and we're here. And we're going to need all the help we can get."

I released the breath I'd been holding since Jed started talking and nodded. We were still a team. I hadn't wrecked our fledgling alliance ... yet.

"Who knows?" Jed continued, pacing around the merry-go-round. "Maybe now that we've found each other, Michael will join us when I'm awake."

He stopped, staring into space like he'd been paralyzed. The play equipment's momentum carried me away from him and I searched the area wildly. No terrors. What had happened to him?

I jumped off the platform and ran to him, grabbing a wrist to check his pulse. "Jed! What's wrong?"

A slow smile spread across his face as he focused his attention on me. I dropped his wrist and waited.

"Yes. It all fits," he said, grasping my upper arms. "You're the reason we're here. Dad didn't ask for this transfer. A letter simply arrived offering him the position. He was going to turn it down. Said he was happy where he was. Then he ... he had this dream ... and suddenly nothing would do but that we move across country to this unheard-of-place in Colorado."

He eased his grip on my arms, but didn't release me. I bent my elbows and clasped his arms as well, locking us together. Into a single unit.

"And who do I meet on my very first day of school," he continued, "in my very first class? You. The only other seer I've ever found." He nodded, his grin broadening. "You see? We were *meant* to find each other."

He stood still as stone for another moment, staring deep into my eyes.

A rushing sound, like wind through a canyon distracted us, bringing with it a noxious odor — bloody and sickly sweet and somehow oily. We released each other and stepped apart, glancing around in panic.

CHAPTER 6

*N*ot one, but three terrors drifted out of the pines and came straight for us.

We'd lowered our guard, forgotten the danger, and now we would pay the price.

I stumbled back a step, grabbed Jed's hand for support, and ducked my head to fall into my trance. Nothing happened.

"Not this time, little girl," the tallest terror whispered, its voice harsh and raspy. "This time we see you."

They glided closer, gnarled, three-fingered, blue-tinged hands outstretched.

My pulse pounded in my ears. Horror clutched my heart. I couldn't concentrate, couldn't find my count. I was visible. They saw me. The terrors would destroy me.

Jed's fingers tightened around mine. He flung out his other hand and shouted, "Begone, foul demons! I command you in the name of Michael the Hunter; leave this place and never return."

The terrors laughed. Horrible scratching noises, like metal gears scraping without benefit of oil.

Jed and I stared at each other. Our powers were useless. We could see our enemy, and they could see us. Fear kindled in his gaze, while it pressed against my throat, strangling me. I grabbed Jed's free hand, stared deep into his eyes, Locked myself in his gaze. My partner. The only person who had ever understood me and accepted me as I was. The one who recognized me, who knew I wasn't crazy.

And suddenly, I understood: I could do anything with Jed by my side.

I ignored the terrors and their putrid smell. Instead, I breathed in the scents of the park, of my natural world, drying grass, pine resin, Jed's musky sweat, and expelled the deep-seated terror of the creatures' unnatural presence; exhaled the panic that had dogged my every breath for every other moment of my life.

Calm rolled across my soul, spreading a soothing balm through my body. My death-grip on Jed relaxed and I smiled. I'd been alone my whole life, but I wasn't alone now. Not when it counted. If death claimed me, I would meet it with a friend.

My new tranquility communicated itself to Jed. An answering light kindled in his eyes. He grinned, squeezed my hands gently, and leaning forward, kissed my forehead. We steadied each other for another heartbeat, and then turned to face the enemy.

"Leave," Jed said, his voice strong and firm. "You have no place in our world."

"Leave," I echoed. "You don't terrify me anymore. I unname you and unmake you. You are no longer terrors."

"Leave," we commanded, united in purpose, in heart, in our very souls.

The creatures stopped. Their arms dropped to their sides, their heads bowed, and then with a wail like the banshee of legend, they faded into oblivion.

Jed pulled me into his arms and squeezed until my ribs hurt, but I didn't complain. I did experience an instant of dizzy unreality — no one but Mom or Dad had ever hugged me before — but the weirdness passed. This wasn't just anyone; this was Jed. My friend.

I settled into his arms, rested my head against his chest, and listened to the steady beat of his heart. We'd done it. My friend and I had conquered terror, and the aftermath felt amazing. Exhilaration mixed with total exhaustion. Every muscle in my body trembled. If Jed hadn't been holding me up, I'd have been a puddle in the drying grass.

After a bit, we parted and, fingers still interlocked, moved to sit again on the merry-go-round.

"We've got work to do," Jed said, stroking the back of my hand with his thumb.

"Agreed." I studied Jed. What a difference a day made. This morning I'd been alone in a new school. A freak. Shunned by my world. Now I was ... what?

Jed smiled at me, a slow lifting of the corners of his mouth coupled with a sparkle in his gray eyes.

I smiled back, and this time it was real, spontaneous. No longer a forced expression of an emotion I didn't understand. Happy. Content. I was both, for the first time in my life. Thanks to Jed, terrors no longer terrified me.

We'd been outcasts most of our lives, but we'd found each other and discovered our purpose. We were soul mates, but not in a mushy romantic way. Two halves of a single whole. Together, we could make a difference.

We would find a safe place to study — maybe the hallowed ground of Reverend Kendrick's church would offer us sanctuary — and we would learn all that Michael could teach.

And someday, when we were ready, we would banish terrors from the face of our good earth. Together.

COPYRIGHT

TERRORS

Copyright © 2018 by Debbie Mumford
First published by WMG Publishing, Inc. March 2016
Published by WDM Publishing
Cover and Layout copyright © 2018 by WDM Publishing
Cover design by WDM Publishing
Cover art copyright © Sellingpix | Dreamstime.com

TO HAVE...AND TO HOLD

PROLOGUE

*M*y name is Artie Woodward, and I'm the happiest girl alive.

Wow! I never thought that phrase would apply to me, especially when I was a kid. I mean, I'm a seer. I see things normal people don't, things they couldn't see, even if they wanted to, which no one in their right mind would. I mean, even I don't want to see the terrors, but I don't have a choice. I was born with this strange ability to see the unseen, to know the unknowable.

I thought I was alone. Thought I'd spend my whole life alone.

Sure, my mom and dad loved me, but even they thought I was weird. They worried about me constantly and dragged me to more shrinks than I care to remember. None of them helped. After all, they all thought I was imagining things. Except I wasn't. So I learned to hide.

I became adept at hiding. I hid my knowledge from my parents. I tried desperately to hide my weirdness from the kids at school. But most importantly, I hid the fact that I could see them, that I knew they existed, from the terrors themselves. And as long as I hid, I stayed safe.

Lonely, but safe.

So how did I grow up to be the happiest girl in the world? How did my life change from hidden and lonely to fulfilled and glowing with contentment?

Jed Kendrick found me.

We recognized each other, and our loneliness ended. We were both seers, and on our first day at McKinley High we became a team, but that's another story. Suffice it to say we've fought terrors together for nearly six years and have developed an unshakable bond.

And along the way, we fell in love.

And now, I'm the happiest girl in the world because in late September I'll become Jed Kendrick's wife, and he'll become Artie Woodward's husband. The Woodward-Kendrick team will be official in the eyes of the world.

But first, we had to make a pilgrimage to Ireland. Jed's grannie insisted.

1

On a beautiful summer day in mid-August, Grannie O'Toole met us at the Dublin airport. We emerged from a sea of people to find her waiting for us, an island of calm in the form of a small, lean woman with frizzy gray hair that Jed assured me had once been curly and deep red.

"Jedidiah Kendrick," she called, opening her arms and stepping toward us with lively impatience. "Come and give your grannie a hug!"

Jed obeyed without hesitation, wrapping the little woman in his long arms and lifting her right off the airport's tiled floor.

"It's so good to see you, Grannie," he said as he placed her gently back on her feet. He grinned like a loon as he released her and angled his body to include me in their conversation. "Grannie, this is Artie, the love of my life." His eyes twinkled as he reached for my hand. "Artie, this is Grannie O'Toole, the best Irish grannie a boy could ever dream of."

Grannie O'Toole reached for my other hand while still maintaining a firm grasp on my husband-to-be. As our fingers met, a circle of energy clicked into place. Suddenly, the three of us really were an island in a sea of people. The pervasive buzz of voices around us muffled, people flowed past us without seeming to notice our existence. We were a rock in the stream that they avoided without awareness.

Grannie nodded. "I wondered," she said, her voice calm and quiet. "I knew Jeremiah was a seer from the moment of his birth." She turned her faded hazel eyes on Jed. "You held the potential, but Jerry held the power. Even here in Ireland, I felt the change when he died and you accepted the mantle."

Jed startled. I felt the slight pull of his fingers on mine, saw his gaze tighten and focus as he stared at his grandmother. "You knew?" he asked. The question held a tinge of accusation, and I heard his unvoiced thought. *You knew what I was and you didn't bother to explain? Left me to discover everything for myself?*

"Aye, child. I knew."

Jed tried to withdraw, to pull away from this woman he thought he'd known, but she held him. She must've been stronger than she looked, for my big, strong man failed to break the continuity of our circle.

"Be at peace, my boy," she said in that calm, quiet voice. "It's part of the curse of our blood that we cannot acknowledge one another until our power is fully developed. I could no more help you to find your way than you'll be able to help the next seer in our line." She turned her attention to me. "But you," she said, "you're a surprise. I wondered about the young woman our Jed had fallen for, worried that she might be Fae. 'Tis why I insisted on meeting before the wedding. If you were less than human, I needed to ensure you revealed your true nature before my boy took vows that would bind him to you for eternity."

I was the one who startled now. Every instinct I owned urged me to hide, as I'd done so effectively before Jed and I found each other, but I willed myself to stillness and looked Grannie O'Toole straight in the eye. She met my gaze without flinching and I read nothing but sincerity and warmth.

"Fae?" I asked. "As in fairies? Are fairies real then?"

Her eyes widened. "Of course they are," she exclaimed. "Are you telling me you've attained the years necessary to contemplate marriage without ever encountering the Fae?"

My jaw dropped and I turned my gaze on Jed. "Is she saying that the terrors are really fairies?" I asked. "I always thought fairies were little winged creatures who danced in mushroom circles and slept on flower petals."

Grannie guffawed, there was no other word for the snort of laughter than emanated from her small body, pulling my attention back to her.

"Sorry," she said. "I can see we've a lot of catching up to do. Let's break this circle and speak of normal things until I get you home. My house is warded, strongly warded, against the Fae. We won't need physical contact there in order to have a private conversation."

And so saying, she broke our contact, as easily as if we'd both been toddlers. While she'd been able to hold me like a vise, I had no more luck clutching her fingers than I would've had capturing a moonbeam. I had the feeling Grannie O'Toole had a lot to teach me.

Thank all that is holy, I was absolutely correct.

*G*rannie O'Toole's house was a charming cottage in the Dublin suburb of Shankill. With its whitewashed walls, jewel-red front door, overhanging thatch roof, and blue window boxes filled to overflowing with red chrysanthemums and white baby's breath, the cottage was everything I'd ever imagined of finding in Ireland. The only thing missing from my perfect vision was its setting. Instead of being surrounded by acres of rolling hills in brilliant shades of emerald green, the little cottage was hemmed in on two sides by neighboring homes and in front by a heavily trafficked cobblestone street.

The three of us piled out of the cab Grannie had hired at the airport and soon stood with our meager baggage — a backpack and duffle for Jed and a carry-on size rolling case for me — in the street in front of Grannie's cottage. As we approached that red door, I felt a slight resistance, as if the house pushed me back to the street. An overwhelming urge to walk past swept over me. I stopped, glanced around, and noted a puzzled expression on Jed's face. He felt it too.

Grannie smiled, placed one hand on the door, then held her

other out to us. "Touch my hand," she encouraged. "Just a finger will do."

When both of us complied, she nodded and said, "Jedidiah Kendrick and Artemis Woodward are welcome in my home. Please, come in."

The resistance vanished, as did my need to walk away.

Of course. Grannie had mentioned that her home was warded against the Fae. Evidently those wards worked against seer blood as well, and Jed and I had now been invited inside their protective shield. I shivered, but held my questions until we were safely inside those innocent looking whitewashed walls.

"I wasn't sure if you'd want to share a room," Grannie said breezily as she led us into a comfortable, lived-in front room. A well-worn sofa upholstered in a tweed fabric the green of budding leaves and heaped with throw pillows in bright jewel tones rested before an authentic fireplace complete with stone hearth and a planed log mantle. Two overstuffed chairs in matching upholstery provided additional seating. "But seeing as you're only handfast and not actually married, I've given you each your own space." She grinned. "That, and I didn't want to give up my own room!"

She led us through a cheery kitchen with white pine cabinets and pretty lace curtains, and up a narrow staircase. I hadn't expected a second floor and found myself on a compact landing between two doors leading to identical small rooms tucked under the cottage's eaves.

"These were originally children's quarters," she explained as Jed and I separated and stowed our luggage in the windowless cells. Each was furnished with a single twin bed covered with a colorful quilt, an old-fashioned washstand complete with basin and ewer, and a drawer unit cunningly built into space beneath the eaves. The sloping roof meant Jed could barely stand in his room, and only near the door. "They're tight, but you'll not be spending much time in them."

We trooped back down the stairs and Grannie completed the tour with a glimpse of her bedroom, spacious and sunny compared to the upstairs rooms, and a shared bath complete with old-fashioned claw-footed tub.

At her insistence, Jed and I settled in the front room while she bustled around the kitchen making tea. Once we were all possessed of steaming cups with a rose patterned plate of short-bread cookies resting on the pine coffee table, Grannie returned to the subject of seers and fairies.

"So," she said, settling into the depths of her overstuffed chair. "Tell me about your experience of the Fae. What did you call them? Terrors?"

I glanced at Jed, waited for him to take the lead.

"That's what Artie named them," he said with a nod in my direction. "She's seen them since birth. Like you said in the airport, I didn't see them until Jerry died. He was the seer, I was just his twin."

Grannie turned to me, her blue eyes seeming to pierce my very soul. "I know Jed's bloodline," she said, "know he inherited his ability from my line, but what about you, young woman? How do you come to see the Fae?"

Grannie's scrutiny unnerved me. Without thinking, I angled my head so that my long dark hair shadowed my face, closed my eyes, and concentrated on hiding, on being invisible. Stillness settled over the room and as I counted my heartbeats, I calmed.

Until Jed placed a hand on my arm.

"It's okay, Artie," he said, his tone soothing and soft. The kind of voice he'd use with a startled horse or a frightened child. "You're safe here. Grannie's no threat. She's family. No need to hide."

I opened my eyes and straightened, grasping Jed's hand and

meeting his gaze. I nodded. "You're right," I said and turned my attention back to Grannie. "I'm sorry. You startled me and I reacted without thinking."

She stared at me a moment longer, then said with a sigh, "You've a powerful defense, Artie. Almost I lost sight of you ... and me a seer. I could feel the power coalescing around you, cloaking you, and even so I nearly lost the knowledge of you."

She glanced around the room, and following her gaze I glimpsed pale runes shimmering above windows and doors and centered on walls before they winked out of sight.

"If it weren't for my wards, I think you'd have succeeded in disappearing from my mind completely." She shuddered and took a sip of tea from the rose patterned cup she still held. After a moment, she continued. "Well, I think we've established you've seer blood. From a very potent bloodline. An ancient bloodline."

"More ancient than ours?" Jed asked.

She nodded. "I've never known a seer with that kind of power, but there are legends..." Another pause while she sipped more tea. I could almost see the thoughts tumbling through her mind as she considered.

"Legends?" Jed prompted when the pause grew lengthy.

"What?" Grannie startled, her eyes widening, as though she'd forgotten our presence. "Oh. Yes. Legends. Among the Fae, there's a legend of a pair who will defend the human race, who will banish the Fae to another realm. Make it impossible for them to feed off our fears and baser instincts. A pair who will free us from them for eternity."

She studied us over the rim of her cup. "I wonder..."

I frowned. "That can't be us. I mean, if we were destined for something, wouldn't someone know? Wouldn't *we* know? And how do you know about Fae legends anyway?"

"It's my family's," she gestured at Jed with the cookie she'd just plucked from the plate, "*our* family's business to know.

We've spied on the Fae for years, kept journals of all we've learned. Journals I'll be handing on to you now, my boy. Now that I've seen for myself that you've the sight and your intended is the right sort as well."

Biting into the shortbread cookie, she chewed, swallowed, and took another sip of tea. "The best thing the Fae could do, if they felt the time of the legend approaching, would be to isolate the families. If your parents, and therefore you," she pointed at me with the half-eaten treat, "were isolated from those of us who know and understand what the Fae are, you'd come into your power without benefit of training. Without understanding our ancient enemy. You'd be weak, and easily destroyed."

"As Jerry was," said Jed, a stricken look marring his features.

"Exactly," Grannie said. "Except for an accident of birth, Artie's partner would've been destroyed and she would've gone to her grave without ever reaching her potential, discovering her destiny."

"But because Jed and Jerry were twins," I said, catching the direction of Grannie's thought, "Jed's potential awakened when Jerry died." I squeezed his hand tightly. "And fate brought us together."

Jed gripped my hand with both of his and gazed into my eyes. "Not fate," he said. "Divine intervention. Don't forget Michael. Don't discount Dad's dream that sent us to Colorado."

"Michael?" Grannie's voice was so sharp I felt like she'd pounced on the name with a tiger's unsheathed claws. "Who is Michael?"

Releasing my hand, Jed leaned forward, elbows on knees, and gazed directly into Grannie's eyes. "Michael, the hunter. The archangel. The commander of God's armies. At least, that's who I've always known him as."

Grannie's eyes narrowed. "And how exactly do you know this Michael?"

"I first saw him when Jerry lay dying. When my sight awoke. Everything changed, and when I looked around, I not only saw the thing that had killed Jerry, but I saw him ... the angel ... Michael, standing behind my father, his eyes full of sorrow and pity. That's actually the only time I've ever seen him when I was awake. Every other time he's come to me in dreams."

"In dreams?" Grannie prompted.

"Yeah. He's used dreams to teach me. To tell me how to fight the monsters, the terrors, as Artie calls them. He's given me strategy and curses or spells to defeat them. I'm pretty sure he's the one who visited Dad in the dream that caused him to move us across the country to Artie's hometown. He knew she needed me. That we needed each other."

She nodded, crossing herself quickly. "An angel. Well, imagine that. And here I thought I'd be the one training you." Dusting the shortbread crumbs from her fingers, she stood, collected our tea cups and turned toward the kitchen. "The pair of you really are special if an archangel has chosen to involve himself." She paused, and glanced back over her shoulder. "Since you've little formal knowledge of the Fae, we'll start your education bright and early in the morning."

3
_____

he next few days were full of wonder. Who'd have guessed that I'd have to go all the way to Ireland to read fairy tales? Of course, these particular tales were true.

Grannie pulled out the family journals and we spent every evening studying the Fae. Jed and I learned about the various races of Fae, about their courts and their powers. We learned the places they were most likely to be found, the hills and rings and raths that covered the British Isles and much of Europe, places Grannie felt sure were portals to that other dimension where their true home lay.

We also learned about ley lines. Lines of power which connected those sites, running in straight lines from point to point and which the Fae traveled in processions ... invisible to all but those with seer blood. If an oblivious human had the misfortune to build a structure across one of those lines, death and destruction followed when the next procession occurred.

During the days, Grannie O'Toole took us to church yards and ruins and circles of standing stones, whatever we'd studied the night before. On one such outing we visited a construction site. All three of us could clearly see the blue ley line shimmering with energy in the morning sun ... and running diagonally through the steel bones of what would someday be an upscale shopping mall on the outskirts of Dublin.

Grannie sighed and shook her head. "'Tis a shame it'll never be completed. The Fae travel this path every year at Samhain. Halloween," she added, correctly interpreting my confused expression. "I tried to warn the owner, but he laughed in my face. Fairy tales are for children, and the gullible, don't you know?"

I shivered, glad I'd be safely home in Colorado long before Halloween came around. The terrors I'd learned to battle at Jed's side were bad enough, but here, in the Old Country, the number and variety of Fae were daunting.

Everywhere we went, we saw Fae. Some were kindly, child-sized brownies caring for domestic animals or lending an unseen hand with household chores; some were tricksters, dwarves and goblins amusing themselves by moving keys or hiding reading glasses; but others rivaled the terrors in their malicious intent, feeding on their victims' positive emotions so that the individuals were left with only distrust and sociopathic thoughts.

Grannie O'Toole cautioned us to act as though we were oblivious to the presence of the Fae, no matter their type.

"Don't see them," she advised. "Whatever you do, never look directly at a Fae. If you must observe them, do so only with sidelong glances or have a reason to look past them. Focus on a bit of the landscape beyond where they stand."

Jed bristled at this advice. "Artie and I don't ignore them. We fight and banish them."

"Maybe at home you can afford to fight," she said with sad resignation. "Colorado must be a wonderful place if there are so few Fae that two young people can fight and win. But not here. Not in their stronghold. There are too many, Jed. You and Artie would be overrun and destroyed — or worse, taken as their playthings — in a heartbeat."

"If we are the legendary pair," Jed argued, "how are we supposed to defend the human race and banish the Fae by pretending we're not what we are?"

Grannie poked a finger in his chest, her expression fierce. "You'll defend our people by lying low until you know enough to fight. Remember Jerry. Remember what happens when a seer tries to do that which he's not yet strong enough to accomplish!"

"That's not fair," Jed said through clenched jaws. His voice was low and controlled, but I heard the anger simmering just beneath the words. "Jerry was a child. I'm an adult."

"Jerry was untrained," she retorted, "and you've only just discovered the existence of the Fae. You didn't even know enough to know what you were battling back home in Colorado."

I stepped between them, placing a hand on Jed's arm. "Enough. You're fighting over how and when to fight."

Grannie stepped back, and Jed turned his gaze on me.

"I don't like letting them get away with things," he said, quietly, but with a sullen edge. "They're hurting people."

"I know," I said, stroking my hand down his arm until I could entwine my fingers with his, "I don't like it much either, but I think Grannie's right. We need to hide our knowledge until we've learned all we can here … and then we need to plan."

He nodded, some of the fire leaving his eyes. "You're right. Whether or not we're the pair in their legend, we won't do anyone any good if we take on more than we can handle right now."

Grannie sighed loudly, but held her peace.

"Let's take a break," I suggested. "We've only got two more days in Ireland. Let's do something fun. Grannie," I said, turning to include her in the conversation again, "there must be something we can do that has a low probability of running into the Fae. What do you suggest?"

Grannie's brow furrowed slightly, then cleared as she nodded and smiled. "That's a grand idea, Artie, but I'm thinking we should take it a step further. Why don't we take a break from each other as well as the learning? I've some errands I've been avoiding, and I'll be surprised if the pair of you wouldn't like a bit of time together without me hanging on your every word."

I opened my mouth to protest, but the twinkle in her eye combined with the happy surprise on Jed's face kept me quiet.

She laughed with delight. "As to where you should go, you might enjoy the Dublin Zoo or the National Botanical Gardens. Both are tourist attractions and full of people, and therefore Fae, but if you wander the less traveled paths, you should be safe enough from their notice."

"That sounds lovely," I agreed.

Jed stepped to Grannie and drew her into a hug. "I'm sorry for picking a fight with you," he said, kissing the top of her frizzy head. "You're right, of course, and an afternoon of sight-seeing will give me a chance to clear my head."

She leaned back and reaching up, patted his cheek. "You're a good boy, Jedidiah Kendrick, and I'm pleased and proud to be your grannie."

Stepping out of his embrace, she swiped tears from her eyes with the back of a hand before using it to make shooing motions at us. "Be gone with you now. You can catch a bus to either the zoo or the gardens at the pub where we had dinner last night. Have a grand time and I'll see you this evening."

Unfortunately, we decided not to catch a bus from the pub in Shankill.

4

I'd just come downstairs from gathering my purse and a light jacket when Jed caught me in his arms.

"Alone at last," he whispered in my ear, and then his lips found mine.

My whole body responded to his kiss. My pulse skyrocketed while butterflies played tag in my belly; my toes even tingled. I was warm and happy and ... home. It didn't matter that we were in Ireland, if Jed and I were together, I was home. They say that "home is where the heart is" ... and Jed was, and always will be, my heart.

We broke the kiss, and I laid my cheek against his chest, listening to the steady beat of his heart. My arms encircled his waist, and his held me close, resting his chin on the top of my head.

"I've missed this," he said. "Time together, just the two of us."

I nodded, rubbing my cheek against the soft cotton of his favorite moss green shirt. "I've enjoyed meeting Grannie," I said quietly, "and I've learned so much, but I'm glad we're going home soon." I straightened, leaning back in his arms to smile up at him. "We've got a wedding to plan!"

He grinned back at me. "We certainly do." A slight crease in his brow signaled a change in subject. "Listen, do you mind if we don't go the tourist route? I'm not in the mood to be squashed on a bus and then mingle with hordes of people."

"Fine by me," I said, stepping out of his arms and catching his hand in mine. "We can see zoo animals and flowers back home."

"Good. Let's just take a walk instead. There's a really cool ruin just through the woods. Mom took Jerry and me there once. I think we were about six during that visit," he mused. "Every other time we saw Grannie, she came to us. Lots more affordable to fly one person across the Atlantic than four ... or even three."

A shiver skittered down my spine, but I associated it with the mention of Jed's dead twin, not with intuition. I wish I'd heeded my subconscious mind's subtle warning.

"That sounds perfect," I said instead. "It's a gorgeous day for a walk."

Jed led me down the street, around the corner, and into a children's play park. On the other side of the manicured lawn, an old growth forest brooded. Grabbing my hand, Jed strode quickly toward the trees. As we approached, an opening in the undergrowth appeared and I saw a path of dark earth strewn with moldering leaf duff.

We stepped under the trees and the village and all its modern sights and sounds faded away. A world of shadowy greens and browns enveloped us; no sound reached our ears but a low breeze moaning through the leafy canopy.

I squeezed Jed's hand, reassured by the warmth of his fingers. He grinned down at me.

"Don't worry," he said, pulling me forward into the forest, "this is nothing. The castle is even spookier."

"Wow," I said. "Way to reassure a girl." I rolled my eyes, but laughed at myself and picked up my pace. No need to make the man feel like he was dragging me to my doom.

The day was warm and the woods were still. I felt a bit like I was walking through a dream. To dispel that illusion, and just for the comfort of hearing his voice, I asked, "So where are we going?"

"There's this really frosty ruin in a meadow just the other side of these woods. It's called Puck's Castle. Jerry and I thought it was great when we were kids."

Sunlight glimmered through the canopy, and I realized we'd reached the edge of the woods. Just beyond the trees lay a paved road with the forest lining one side and a low rock wall on the other. We crossed to a metal gate and I had my first sight of the ruin.

Puck's castle looked like a giant's face, mouth open in horror, eyes slitted against a wind only it could feel. A cap of green hair trailed across one corner of its brow.

I shivered. "Why is it called Puck's Castle?"

Jed glanced from the stacked rock ruin to me. "You know, I hadn't thought about that, but I remember now," his brow creased in a frown. "It's supposed to be haunted by a pookah, a mischievous fairy who plays the pipes and hops around on the rocks."

That was when I noticed the muted glow of the ley line.

I grabbed Jed's hand, tugging him back toward the cover of the trees. "We have to go, Jed," I said, trying desperately to mask the hysteria rising in my chest. "Now. We have to go NOW!"

The glow of the ley line was no longer muted. The iridescent blue brightened as I watched, pulsing as though to a musical beat.

Jed ignored my panicked tug. He stared across the meadow to the forest on the far side of the castle.

"Jed," I cried. "Please!"

If he heard me, or felt me yanking on his hand, he gave no sign. My love, the man I intended to marry, stood as though turned to stone and stared as a troop of fairies left the shelter of the woods and marched along the ley line straight to Puck's Castle.

Too late, I thought. *Leaving now will only draw their attention to us.* So I did what I had always done, I hid in plain sight. And prayed that my gift would shield Jed as well.

I peered through the curtain of my dark hair, watching the approaching fairies through slitted eyes. One of their number peeled off and scampered up the rock tower, lithe as a mountain goat. When he reached the top, he danced from stone to stone, lightly skipping over the ivy that trailed in a glistening stream across one corner. His dance ended abruptly on our side of the castle, and I knew I'd been unsuccessful. The pookah saw us ... or at least one of us.

His surprised cry caused the troop to halt, and me to close my eyes and redouble my effort to hide.

But my attempt was in vain.

Footsteps pattered across the green carpeted meadow, and I cracked my eyes open by the merest sliver to see the pookah and two tall, silver-haired companions standing on the other side of the gate from us.

Jed shook his hand loose from mine, as if I were no more than a bothersome fly, and stepped toward the fairies.

"Begone," he said. "You're not wanted here."

"How unusual," said the pookah. "This mortal has eyes that see."

"Unusual and unacceptable," said one of his silver-haired friends. The creature crooked a finger at Jed and said, "Come, mortal. You must meet our queen."

My Jed, my partner, the love of my life, placed a booted foot on the lowest rail of the gate and began to climb over, his eyes glazed, his expression vacant.

I couldn't stand still. I couldn't let them take my Jed!

Flinging my invisibility away, I grabbed Jed's arm. "Jedidiah Kendrick, hear me! Come away, Jed. Come away with me now!"

The three fairies startled, stepping back a pace.

"What's this?" cried the pookah. "From whence did this mortal appear?"

"She holds great power," said the second.

"No matter," said the third, the one who had held silent until now. He turned gleaming orange eyes on me and spoke directly to my soul. "Come. Your will is mine. Follow where I lead."

I barely had time to duck my chin and close my eyes before his words wove their spell. A nearly irresistible urge to climb the gate and follow Jed into the meadow flooded my heart and soul. But a sliver of my will had managed to hide, and that sliver fought the fairy's compulsion. If I fell under his spell, who would rescue Jed?

The thought of losing myself wasn't nearly as terrifying as the thought of losing Jed.

That sliver of self blazed with fear for my love, and the hot emotion broke the fairy's hold on my mind. I slipped into my own spell and the creatures forgot my existence. Jed was their one and only prey.

When the troop had passed, I sank to the ground and sobbed, grieving for the life we'd never share now. I'd been powerless to protect Jed, and my heart ached with loss.

----

*G*rannie was inconsolable. She paced the floor in front of the hearth and wailed her despair, while I held myself together, folded into one of the overstuffed chairs.

"He watched them cross the field? He stood there bold as brass and stared at a procession of fairies?" Her eyes were red with weeping and her voice scratched and cracked as though she'd inhaled a lifetime's cigarette smoke. "Did he learn nothing from me?"

She pulled her already frizzy hair, and then turned on me. "And you ... how did you come home again, lassie? How are you here and not my Jedidiah?"

My own tears were gone, washed away in the flood I'd shed on the lane outside Puck's Castle. I had nothing left to give.

"I hid," I said. "I tried to shield him too, but they saw him anyway."

"You hid," she said, the words dripping scorn. "You claim to love my boy, but you did naught to save him. You hid."

"I tried," I answered, stung by the injustice of her accusation. "I cast away my protection and tried to call him back. He loves me. I love him." I sighed, futility washing over me yet again. "I thought my call would be stronger than theirs. I was wrong."

"Then how are you here?"

"I realized it wasn't working," I explained. "My sudden appearance startled them, gave me just enough time to slip back into my trance." I closed my eyes and rested my head in my hands. "Even so, I almost didn't make it. The only thing that saved me was the knowledge that Jed was lost if I gave in."

Her hand settled on my hair and stroked; the touch comforted me.

"I'm sorry, Artie," she whispered. "This is none of your doing and 'tis wrong of me to lay blame at your feet."

I rose and hugged her tightly. "I'm so sorry," I whispered. "I don't know what to do."

We separated, staring at each other through bleak eyes.

"How do we get him back?"

Grannie closed her eyes and sank onto the sofa, pulling me down beside her. "Oh, child," she said. "He's lost and there's nothing we can do about it."

I bristled, hot anger replacing despair. "I can't accept that," I said. "I won't accept that. I need him. We need each other. There has to be a way to steal him back."

She patted my arm. "I've never heard of the Fae releasing one of their toys," she said, but something in my expression made her change tack. "We'll search the old texts. Not just our family journals, but those in the clan library."

"Is yours the only seer clan?"

Grannie pursed her lips and thought. "I know a few other families. I'll ask them to search their journals as well."

I nodded, suddenly too weary to hold up my head. Research. It wasn't much, but it was hope, and I would cling to hope until I could cling to Jed again.

"Go to bed, Artie," Grannie said with a pat on my knee. "Neither of us is thinking clearly at the moment. We'll start our search in the morning."

I nodded and found my way to the second floor, where I was now the only occupant.

6

Our search was long and arduous, but Grannie O'Toole was a steadfast guide. We read every word of her family journals before moving to the headquarters of her ancestral clan, the O'Connors, and petitioning to search their library.

Fortunately, the O'Connor library was located in Dublin. Unfortunately, the older texts were indecipherable to me, and eventually proved beyond Grannie's skill at translation as well.

Days dragged by, followed by plodding weeks of reading ancient script until my eyes ached. Family and friends in Colorado called asking when Jed and I were coming home. I prevaricated, misled, and outright lied. I couldn't bear to tell anyone that he'd been stolen, kidnapped by supernatural creatures. No one would believe me anyway, so I hid behind a façade of a holiday too delightful to bring to a close.

August's myriad greens turned to the golds and reds of September with no solution in sight. Despair seized me by the throat as our anticipated wedding date approached ... and passed with me no nearer to rescuing Jed. I couldn't go on like this. I couldn't live without him, but I couldn't give up while he might be saved. Maybe the next document would hold the secret. I kept searching

By mid-October we had reached the limits of our ability to research, and I was desperately afraid I'd be forced to leave Ireland ... to abandon the possibility of ever seeing my love again.

Just when our spirits had reached their lowest ebb, Laird Angus O'Connor sought us out. He found us in a dim library chamber where tattered scrolls and decaying journals lined shelves set against stone walls dark with age. An ancient oak table occupied the center of the room, its wood so stained and dark it seemed to absorb what little light filtered through the high, narrow windows. The most ancient scrolls dealing with the Fae resided in this room ... scrolls filled with script that had defied even Grannie's ability to read.

The clan leader was an impressive man, with a broad chest, heavily muscled arms, a thick neck, and a full head of deep auburn hair. Though he was clean shaven and wearing a perfectly tailored suit, he looked like a warrior of legend.

"Maeve O'Toole," he called in a booming voice that filled the narrow chamber. "I've heard tales that you and your young assistant have fair taken up residence among the journals of our clan. Do you seek specific knowledge, or are you merely broadening your understanding of your heritage?"

Grannie scrambled to stand, so I followed suit, but when she gave the man a low bow, I merely inclined my head. He was not my laird, nor was he ever likely to become so, the way our search was going.

"Laird," said Grannie, standing as tall as her slight frame would allow. "We're looking for specific information ... regarding the Fae."

"I see." He shot a piercing look at me, and I saw wariness and a shrewd intelligence in his gaze. "And who might your assistant be? If she's of our clan, I've no recollection of her."

Grannie folded her hands in front of her and lowered her gaze. "She is not of our clan … yet. Laird Angus O'Connor, may I present Artemis Woodward. Artie, this is my clan leader, Angus O'Connor."

Laird Angus held out a massive hand, and I laid mine in it.

"'Tis pleased I am to make your acquaintance, Miss Woodward," he said, lifting my hand and brushing my knuckles with his lips. As he did so, a flash of recognition seared my mind. This man was not only a seer, he was far older than his looks suggested.

He smiled, a twinkle lighting his eyes. "Ah, I see your blood recognizes mine. Good. That will expedite matters." He released my hand, sat down at the long narrow table between the racks of books and scrolls, and gestured us to chairs as well. "What do you seek, and how may I assist you?"

Grannie raised an eyebrow in my direction, but remained silent. I sighed. I preferred to leave the explaining to her, but obviously she'd decided this was my tale to tell.

"Very well," I said, and gave my full attention to the laird of the O'Connors. "I'm engaged to Mrs. O'Toole's grandson, Jedidiah Kendrick. We came to Ireland so that Grannie could meet me before we married. Once here, we discovered that Grannie is a seer, like Jed and myself. However, we found Grannie to be much more knowledgeable, so we set out to learn what we could from her before we returned home to the United States, to our home in Colorado."

I told Laird Angus everything I could, every detail of how Jed had been taken and how I'd escaped. The telling was hard. During the weeks Grannie and I had searched for answers, I'd tried not to think about that day, tried not to remember exactly how I'd failed Jed. Instead, I'd concentrated on finding a solution. But it had all been in vain.

Grannie and I avoided speaking of the future. I lived in her house and we worked side by side searching the records for clues, but I knew in my heart I couldn't stay in Ireland forever. Yet, I couldn't imagine returning to Colorado without Jed. Frankly, I couldn't imagine living without Jed. If I left the Old Country without him, what point would there be for my existence?

And so I stayed, would continue to stay, until I found Jed or Grannie sent me away.

As I finished my tale, Laird Angus took my hands in his and stroked them with his thumbs. Compassion filled his gaze as he said, "Ah, lassie, 'tis sorry I am to hear of your woes, but the chances of you regaining your love are very slim."

Tears filled my eyes, but I blinked them back. "I know," I whispered. "Actually, they're about gone since even Grannie can't decipher these final journals."

"I can see you're a steadfast lass," he said, releasing my hands, "but have you courage as well as loyalty?"

I swiped at my eyes to clear the tears and met his gaze. "I've dealt with terror since my earliest memories, and did it on my own until Jed found me. We were in our teens by then. Together he and I fought the terrors, the Fae ... and won. Until we came here." I lowered my eyes and studied the delicate opal ring Jed had given me when we agreed to marry. "There are so many more Fae here, and we had so very much to learn. I guess we failed."

Laird Angus lifted my chin with his index finger until my eyes met his. "I may know a way," he said, "but you'll have to act alone, and it will require more courage than most seers possess. I'll not fault you if you choose to leave this place with the tale untold."

My heart leaped. My pulse thundered so hard I could barely hear past its whooshing against my eardrums. "Y... you ... you know how get Jed back? Tell me," I demanded. "Tell me now!"

"Oh, Laird!" Grannie said, and she looked so white I worried she might faint.

The big man laughed. "Call me Angus," he said. "We've no need for formalities between us. We're seers all, with much work to be done."

The plan was simple to tell, yet seemed impossible to execute.

As Angus explained, all I had to do was pull Jed out of line as the fairy troop processed along a ley line during a full moon ... and hold him until he recognized me.

"You can see them, so you can do it," Angus assured me.

"It sounds too easy," I said, frowning. "What's the catch?"

His eyes darted around the room as he looked for something to focus on that wasn't me. "The catch, as you say, is that you must hold him no matter what the fairies do. No matter what spell they throw at you." He sighed and met my gaze. "Their own laws dictate that they cannot harm you during the rescue attempt, but if you despair, if you lose hold of him for even an instant, both of you will be lost beyond recovery."

"Beyond recovery?" Grannie said, and I heard the fear and tension in her voice. "What does that even mean?"

"Exactly what it says, Maeve," Angus answered. "Only one attempt is permitted for Jed, and since Artie will be attempting to steal from the Fae, no attempts will be tolerated on her behalf. Either they both come home, or neither does."

I nodded, then made eye contact with each in turn. "That suits me fine. If I can't save Jed, I've no reason to go on."

Angus nodded, a fierce glare in his eyes. Grannie's eyes brimmed with tears, but she bit her lip and made no objection.

7

_H_alloween, or Samhain as the Celts called it, brought the next full moon.

Grannie and Angus prepared for the attempted rescue by creating a shield bracelet for me and embedding it with every protective sigil and ward they could discover. Angus also took my engagement ring and sealed it with a spell to enhance the love it represented.

"We can't go with you," he explained, "can't help you with this task, but we can see to it you carry as much positive energy with you as is physically possible."

I spent my preparation time writing down everything I could remember of the time Jed and I had spent together. From our first meeting in social studies on our first day of high school, through every battle with every terror we'd ever vanquished, right down to the way he'd kissed me before we walked to Puck's Castle on that fateful day. Those memories strengthened me. They reminded me of all we'd accomplished, of all we'd become to one another.

Jed was my life and I was his. No matter what, I would hold him. Nothing a fairy or a terror or any other foul thing that walked our earth could do would cause me to abandon my man. Jed was the other half of my soul and I refused to continue to be separated from him.

Halloween morning dawned clear and bright and biting with cold. The time had come. Tonight the moon would be full and the fairy troop that had stolen Jed would process right through the middle of an under-construction mall on the outskirts of Dublin ... the one Grannie had shown us early in our visit.

"You're sure it's the same troop?" I asked, wiping damp palms on my well-worn denim jeans. "If he's not there, we'll have to wait for the next full moon."

"I'm certain, Artie," Angus said. "I've had spies out for the last few weeks. Experienced seers who know how to watch without being caught. Jed is with this troop, and except for being completely enthralled, he is whole and well."

I nodded, busying my fingers with binding my long dark hair in a single tight braid. I'd have no need to hide behind my hair this night. "Good. That's good."

"Come, Artie," Grannie called from the kitchen. "Let me fix you a nice dinner. You'll need your strength tonight."

I shook my head, remembered she couldn't see through walls, and called back, "No thank you, Grannie. I'm too nervous to eat. Besides, I'm stronger than I look. I'll be fine."

She hurried in to the front room a few minutes later carrying a tray of steaming mugs. "I thought that might be your attitude," she said with a wan smile. "Here, at least drink this broth. It'll fortify you without weighing you down."

"Good thinking, Maeve," Angus said with an approving nod, accepting his own mug. "Drink up, Artie. It'll be time to leave before you know it."

Angus and Grannie drove me to the construction site, timing it so we arrived just as the moon rose full and bright above the horizon. Grannie hugged me and wished me well, while Angus touched my ring and bracelet. "You're well warded, lassie, and ye've a stout heart. I've no doubt ye'll prevail."

I nodded and spoke past the lump in my throat. "We'll see you soon. Both of us." I licked lips that felt more like sandpaper than flesh. "But, if anything goes wrong, you have our story. Add it to your journal, please."

"There'll be no need, at least not until you've added another fifty years' worth of tales."

A quick grin and I left them to hide myself behind a pallet of bricks that was stacked beside the shining ley line. All that remained to be done was to wait for my love, my life, my Jed.

The moon floated just above the horizon, so round and full it seemed to fill the sky. A shining white orb starred with mars and craters against a velvet black sky studded with pinpricks of light. Surely such beauty boded well for Jed's rescue.

A soft jingle of bells wafted across the silent night. They were coming.

I hunkered low in a sprinter's crouch, one eye on the ley line, ready to spring the moment I saw him. My pulse raced, my vision wavered, my ears rang with nerves.

The first fairy appeared. An ageless female in a flowing green gown holding aloft a branch of silver leaves threaded with tiny golden bells. Behind her came a tall raven-haired male garbed all in deep blue carrying a purple banner trimmed in golden threads. Next came a throng of fair folk, easily thirty or forty individuals of all species, including a few Grannie hadn't described. Another bannerman and bell-bearer brought up the rear.

He wasn't there! Jed wasn't part of the procession!

How could we have been so wrong? What could I do now?

I closed my eyes against a suffocating wave of despair. And

then I heard the clip-clop of horses' hooves on the moon-drenched ground.

My eyes flew open and I beheld a snow white unicorn following the final bell-bearer. The ethereal creature had appeared as if out of thin air, and sitting sideways upon his back was the most beautiful lady I could ever have imagined. The female was dressed in gossamer fabrics, like moonbeams on an icy lake, in shimmering shades of palest blue, rose-petal pink and tender green. Her face and form were perfectly proportioned, an alabaster complexion framed emerald green eyes and her hair had the shade and shine of molten gold.

Surely this must be the fairy queen the pookah had spoken of, I couldn't imagine her as anything else.

My heart leapt and my soul stilled almost before I realized what I had seen. Jed walked beside the queen's horse, his hand resting lightly on her slipper clad foot, his eyes glazed and unaware.

My moment had arrived.

I sprinted from my hiding place, knocking Jedidiah to the ground. Encircling his left wrist with my right hand, I threw my left arm around his neck and clung to him like a burr.

Jed spoke not a word, but lay like a mannequin on the ground beneath me. Could it be this easy? Could I have won already?

Almost I loosened my grip, but the ring on my left hand and bracelet on my right flared to life and I felt their protective sigils glow.

No, I hadn't won. I'd merely surprised my enemy. The battle had yet to be engaged.

The fairy queen called out in ringing tones more beautiful than I could describe. The troop stopped. All eyes focused on me ... and Jed.

Unpronounceable, unknowable words tumbled from the queen's lips … and my reality transformed.

I no longer held Jed. Instead I clung to the head of a giant snake that raised itself … and me … into the sky. I closed my eyes and chanted a mantra to the man I knew I held though the evidence of my senses told me otherwise. "You are Jedidiah Kendrick and I am Artemis Woodward. I love you and you love me. Come back to me, Jed!"

The weaving head faltered, the massive jaw closed, and a huge forked tongue darted out, tasting my scent upon the air between us.

The fairy queen spoke again, commandment in every unknown syllable.

The snake shifted and I no longer clung to smooth scales. Now my left arm wrapped the coarsely furred neck of a Bengal tiger, while my right hand fought to hold its claws from my flesh. Golden eyes stared at the pulse in my naked throat and knife-sharp teeth gleamed in its open mouth.

I closed my eyes and held on still more tightly. No matter what form the fairy queen forced upon him, I refused to release my Jed. If she made him kill me, so be it. I'd rather die than fail him again.

Fear clogged my throat, but I opened my eyes, stared straight into his, and screamed, "You are Jedidiah Kendrick and I am Artemis Woodward. I love you and you love me. Come back to me, Jed!"

The tiger's claws relaxed and something flickered behind his eyes.

The fairy queen spoke again, her words strident and somehow desperate.

Jed writhed and bucked beneath my hands, but I refused to release him. When the transformation was complete, I found myself eye to eye with the biggest bird I'd ever seen. My left arm encircled his neck, pulling a razor sharp beak too close to my face, while my right hand held tight to the pinion of his left wing.

Intelligence flashed behind his eyes as he cocked his great head and blinked a nictitating membrane. I smiled, with more courage than I felt, and repeated, for the third time, "You are Jedidiah Kendrick and I am Artemis Woodward. I love you and you love me. Come back to me, Jed!"

He lowered his feathered head, touching my forehead with his own.

"I love you, Jed Kendrick," I whispered, "and I will never let you go."

The fairy queen spoke again, but this time her voice held defeat. The great bird that had been Jed deflated and morphed and became ... Jedidiah Kendrick, a mortal man with his two feet planted firmly on the ground.

Jed stared into my eyes from where we stood, my right hand in his left, my left arm flung around his neck. He raised his right hand and caught the tear sliding down my cheek on his index finger. "I see you, Artemis Woodward. I know you. You are the love of my life."

Neither of us even glanced up when the fairy queen spoke. We had eyes only for each other.

"Congratulations, mortal female," she said, her voice distant and cool. "By the terms of our law you have won back my thrall. He is free from this troop, but I warn you, do not linger on these shores for all of my other troops will be anxious to avenge this slight. I now know both of your names and I do *not* wish you well."

Jed and I held each other without speaking until the troop had disappeared and Grannie and Angus ran to embrace us.

EPILOGUE

*T*hanksgiving is a uniquely American holiday and Jed and I celebrated it in Colorado with our families ... by pledging our lives to each other. Since our ordeal in Ireland had given us so much to be thankful for, we decided Thanksgiving was the perfect day for our wedding.

Grannie O'Toole arrived the day before, accompanied by Angus O'Connor. Jed was honored beyond words that the head of the O'Connor clan would come all the way to America just to attend our wedding.

I'd explained how Angus had been instrumental in Jed's rescue, but my love remained vague about the weeks of his captivity. Everything I told him of that time seemed to slip from his mind as soon as I said it, but I didn't mind. In fact, I envied him his forgetfulness. If I could erase the memory of my despair and grief, I'd do it gladly, except that it would also erase my knowledge of Grannie's steadfast support and how hard Angus had worked to help me bring Jed home.

The ceremony itself was a small affair. Jed and I exchanged our vows in the little neighborhood park where we'd first become a team. I wore a clean-lined white velvet dress, full length and long-sleeved in deference to the late November chill, and carried a small bouquet of gold asters and wine-red chrysanthemums. Jed looked regal in a black tux and a cummerbund, the latter in a deep gold shade that matched his aster boutonniere. Reverend Kendrick, Jed's father, officiated, and our vows were witnessed by Jed's mother, my parents, and Grannie and Angus.

Reverend Kendrick's face fairly glowed as he recited the age-old words, "Jedidiah Amos Kendrick, do you take Artemis Lucia Woodward to be your wedded wife, to love, protect, and cherish, to have and to hold from this day until the end of time?"

A slow smile spread across Jed's face, lighting his eyes and making him even more handsome than usual. He squeezed my hands. "I certainly do."

His father turned his gaze on me. "And do you, Artemis Lucia Woodward, take Jedidiah Amos Kendrick to be your wedded husband, to love, protect, and cherish, to have and to hold from this day until the end of time?"

The memory of those moments when the fairy queen had transformed my love from one deadly form to the next flitted through my mind. I had held him then, I would hold him forever.

"I do," I said without a single doubt.

Jed pulled me into his embrace and our lips met in a kiss that caused everything around us to fade into the background. I'm sure his father intoned the final words of the ceremony, but I didn't hear them. I didn't need to.

I was Jed's and he was mine ... and there wasn't a terror or a fairy in sight.

What could be more perfect?

COPYRIGHT

TO HAVE...AND TO HOLD
Copyright © 2018 by Debbie Mumford
Published by WDM Publishing
Cover and Layout copyright © 2018 by WDM Publishing
Cover design by WDM Publishing
Cover art copyright © <u>Whiteisthecolor</u> | <u>Dreamstime.com</u>

SELKIES IN PARADISE

PROLOGUE

 *M*y name is Artie Woodward-Kendrick, and I'm the luckiest woman in the world. I'm married to my very best friend, Jed Kendrick.

Who could've guessed I'd ever find someone to love; that I would ever marry? Certainly not me!

You see, I'm a seer. I see things normal people don't, things they couldn't see, even if they wanted to ... which no one in their right mind would. I mean let's get real; even I don't want to see the Fae. But I don't have a choice. I was born with this strange ability to see the unseen, to know the unknowable.

I thought I was alone. Thought I'd be alone my entire life. I knew I'd never find love.

Sure, my mom and dad loved me, but even they thought I was weird. They worried about me constantly when I was a kid, dragged me to more shrinks than I care to remember. None of them helped. After all, everyone assumed I was imagining things.

Only I wasn't.

So I learned to hide.

By the time I made it to high school, I was adept at hiding. I hid my knowledge from my parents. I tried desperately to hide my weirdness from the kids at school. But most importantly, I hid the fact that I could see what I'd named *the terrors*, that I knew they existed, from the terrors themselves. And as long as I hid, I was safe.

Lonely ... but safe.

So how did I manage to find a man who not only befriended me, but who grew to love me? How did my life change from hidden and lonely to fulfilled and glowing with contentment?

Jed Kendrick moved to my hometown in Colorado.

We recognized each other, and our loneliness ended. We were both seers, and on our first day at McKinley High we became a team, but that's another story. Suffice it to say that over the last six and a half years we've fought terrors and other forms of Fae from Colorado to Ireland.

And somewhere along the way, we fell in love.

Now, I'm glowing with happiness because just a few days ago, on a glorious late November day — Thanksgiving Day to be exact — I became Jed Kendrick's wife, and he became Artie Woodward's husband. The Woodward-Kendrick team became official in the eyes of the world.

What's next, you ask? Who knows! But whatever it is, we'll face it together.

Right after we get home from the awesome honeymoon our family and friends arranged for us ... in Hawaii!

1

On a crystal clear day in late November, our plane landed in paradise. Aside from a fateful trip to Ireland to meet Jed's Grannie O'Toole, I'd never been beyond the borders of Colorado, so when I stepped from the plane into the open-air terminal at Lihui Airport on the Hawaiian island of Kauai, I was overwhelmed. I stopped in the midst of a throng of people, clinging to Jed's arm, and inhaled the exotic mixture of sea salt, tropical flowers, and lushly green growing things.

Jed squeezed my hand and smiled down at me. "We're here," he said, his voice tinged with amazement. "We're actually married and on our honeymoon."

I nodded, momentarily lost in the love and wonder shining in his eyes. There had been moments in Ireland when I'd despaired of ever seeing Jed's handsome face again, and now here we were ... married and on the island of Kauai.

Before I could answer, a pretty young woman with a waterfall of shining black hair and sun-kissed skin stepped up to us. She wore a sleeveless red dress patterned with huge white flowers, and her arms dripped with brightly colored flower leis.

"Aloha," she said as she placed a lei around each of our necks. "Welcome to Kauai. We hope you'll enjoy your stay."

I smiled my thanks, but my attention was caught by the beauty of the flowers that made up my lei. I'd never seen, or smelled, anything like them. I recognized white carnations in the necklace of flowers, but the other varieties were a mystery.

I glanced up and met her gaze. "Thank you. These are beautiful, but what kind of flowers are they?"

She held up another of the leis she carried and indicated a white, star-like flower edged in delicate pink. "This is plumeria. Most of the fragrance of your lei comes from it. You'll see them often here in the islands. Sometimes in pink, often in yellow." Pointing to other flowers in turn she said, "We also use tuberoses, carnations, orchids, and jasmine, but you'll see many other types of leis during your stay." She smiled again, and with a little wave, turned to greet another couple.

Jed fingered the lei around his neck — his was made up of darker, more bold colors than mine and featured quite a bit of greenery — and said, "Wow. I didn't expect to be given flowers just for walking off a plane."

"They look good on you," I said, grinning up at my tall, lanky husband. I'd nearly lost Jed in Ireland. He'd been ensorcelled and held thrall by the Fae, and I'd almost given up hope of finding a way to rescue him. But Grannie O'Toole and Laird Angus had helped me and ... well, that was a tale I didn't want to think about right now.

It was enough to have him here with me, to be able to watch him examine his lei while I admired his more-than-six-foot frame, his tousled black hair, and his gentle gray eyes rimmed by long and lovely dark lashes. His full lips twitched as he noticed my stare.

"Like what you see?" he asked, his eye color darkening to a smoldering, smoky gray.

"Always," I replied, my heart beating faster as memories of our wedding night crowded my mind. "Let's find our luggage."

"Yes," he agreed, licking his lips. "I think we need to check out our accommodations." He swallowed, his Adam's apple bobbing. "Soon."

2

Our hotel suite was stunning. The laird had gone all out for us after our Irish misadventure. He'd booked us into a luxury resort on Kauai's north shore and made sure we had all the amenities. I wandered through the sitting room and stepped through the sliding glass door onto the ocean-view lanai, while Jed tipped the young man who'd brought our luggage up.

A soft murmur of voices, the muffled thump of a closing door, and a moment later Jed was beside me, his arms sliding around my waist. We gazed at the picture postcard view of palm trees, white sand and impossibly blue water and then turned to each other.

"Welcome to paradise," Jed murmured as he drew me close and bent to kiss me.

His lips were soft and warm, and I melted into his embrace. Jed loved me. He understood me. He was my partner in life, my equal. And now ... right now, he was my lover.

Our kiss deepened, became more passionate, and when the spark it kindled grew to a flame, he pulled away. The light in his eyes echoed the smoldering heat growing in my core. In one quick movement, he bent and, moving one strong arm behind my knees, swept me off my feet and into his arms. Without a word, my lover carried me across the sitting room and into the bedroom ... to the perfectly arranged and very enticing king-size bed.

"You're wearing too many clothes," he whispered as he placed me gently on the pillow-soft mattress.

"So are you," I answered in voice so husky I barely recognized it as my own.

We remedied that little problem and spent the next few hours doing what newlyweds have done since time immemorial: exploring each other's bodies and discovering new depths of our love.

Our first day on Kauai was drawing to a close when we emerged from our hotel suite in search of food. We opted for dinner on the terrace overlooking Hanalei Bay. I watched the sun sink into the darkening water, marveling at the vivid shades of red and gold as I savored firm, sweet flakes of mahi mahi flavored with mango sauce and delicious coconut rice.

Jed caught my free hand in his, stroking my fingers with his thumb. We didn't speak. No words were needed. We simply drank in the moment, appreciating the tranquility and peace of this beautiful place.

After dinner, we wandered through the open air hotel lobby and down a stone-paved path to a pristine white sand beach. The rolling waves of the bay beckoned us with their froth of white lace.

We strolled hand-in-hand in the moonlight, serenaded by the susurrus of water on sand, cooled by a light sea breeze that lifted my long dark hair and ruffled Jed's black locks. As we rounded the curve of the bay, I noticed a woman in a long white dress sitting in the sand at the edge of the water. Her knees were pulled up so that her chin rested on them, the gentle waves kissing her feet with each inward flow. We walked a few steps closer, and she raised her head and glanced at us. Moonlight shimmered on her face, and I saw that it was glazed with tears.

I laid my free hand on Jed's arm to stop him, disentangled my fingers from his, and stepped nearer to the woman. Closer now, I saw that she was young, not much older than me, with lovely dark slanting eyes. But the moonlight played tricks with her hair, making the nearly waist-length sable waves appear to have a silvery sheen.

"Are you hurt?" I asked, just loudly enough to be heard over the waves. "Can we help you?"

And then Jed was beside me, pulling me back toward the resort. "Come away from her, Artie," he whispered urgently in my ear. "Can't you see what she is?"

I looked again, and saw what my love had seen.

The young woman had risen. She stood with her feet in a froth of water, her long white dress wet to the knees, one hand held out to us in a gesture of supplication. An unearthly glow surrounded her, one not detectable by normal human eyes ... but neither Jed nor I were normal humans. We were seers. And right now our sight showed us a woman of the Fae.

"Please," she said, making no move to approach us. "Please, can you help me?"

Jed pushed me behind him, but made no move to flee. "What could a mortal do to help a Fae woman?"

She gasped and stumbled back a step. "Y-you know what I am?"

I stepped to Jed's side, despite his annoyed glance. "Not precisely," I said. "Only that you aren't human."

Nodding, she moved closer, hesitantly, like a wild animal. Curious, but cautious. And always with her feet in the waves.

"I'm a selkie," she said, her dark eyes wide and full of pain, "but I can't return home to the sea. Someone has stolen my skin. I'm marooned here, with no one to tell my kin what has become of me. Can you help me? Can you at least carry a message to my colony?"

A selkie. One of that ancient race of shape-shifters who live in the oceans of the world, appearing to human eyes as seals in the water, and transforming into human form on land. But the transformation required a catalyst. To become human, a selkie had to shed its skin, which was then carefully hidden. Very carefully, because without its skin, the creature was powerless to shift into its true form and return to the water.

"We've learned to distrust the Fae," Jed said, his voice low and menacing. "My wife may be sympathetic, but I won't risk her on what could be a trick."

Tears streamed across her cheeks as she shook her head. "It's no trick. I'm desperate, and you're the only ones who can possibly understand my plight. Please, help me." She wiped her cheeks with trembling hands, took a deep breath, and continued. "If you won't seek out my kin, at least tell Maris where I am and what has happened."

"Who?" Jed and I asked simultaneously.

"Maris Grainger," said the selkie woman. "She lives on Maui. I have no money and I can no longer swim, so I can't reach her. Go to Maui, to Maalaea Harbor. Look for Captain Bill's Island Cruises. Her father works there. He'll tell you how to find Maris. Tell her Serena needs her help. She'll go to my family. Maris will know what to do."

I frowned. "Is she a seer?" I asked, confused. "How can this Maris Grainger help you?"

"Maris is special," she said. "Different. Neither Fae nor human, but she's kind and cares for all who inhabit the sea.

She'll help. She'll know what to do. Please, tell Maris Serena needs her."

Jed and I exchanged a glance. We'd planned to do some sight-seeing on Maui anyway, and an island cruise sounded lovely. I quirked an eyebrow at him and he shrugged his shoulders in a *might as well* kind of way. I grinned and stood on tiptoe to kiss his cheek.

"We'll see if we can find Maris tomorrow," I said.

The selkie nodded. "Thank you."

Jed and I turned and practically ran back to the resort.

"Well, that's a first," Jed said quietly when we were safely back in the open air lobby. "A member of the Fae asking for our help."

I nodded. Every other encounter we'd ever had with that race of supernatural creatures had been hostile. As we took the elevator to our suite, I wondered what manner of being this Maris Grainger might be. Not Fae. Not human. Then what exactly was she?

Evidently a being who was kind and cared for sea creatures.

How intriguing!

3

_____

he next morning we caught an island hopper flight to Kapalua Airport on Maui, rented a red Jeep Wrangler, and drove to Maalaea Harbor. What a wonderfully adventurous start to our day! Flying over the emerald jewel of Kauai and the diamond-tipped sapphire of the Pacific before landing on Maui's northwest coast. We drove south along Highway 30, the open-topped Wrangler giving us clear views of the ocean to the west and the stunning West Maui Mountains to the east.

We arrived in Maalaea Town a little before noon and went in search of Captain Bill's Island Cruises. The young woman manning the ticket booth told us that the Graingers sailed on the Sea Princess, which was currently on a whale watching run, but that we could book seats on the Sea Princess for its 2:00 p.m. snorkeling cruise.

Jed pulled out the credit card Laird Angus had provided and paid for our afternoon adventure. The young woman advised us to be back by 1:30 to board the Sea Princess and grab choice seats.

Pushing his wallet back into his pocket, Jed turned to me.

"Shall we find some lunch? We've got a little over an hour to kill."

As if on cue, my stomach growled, loudly.

"I'll take that as a 'yes,'" Jed said with a laugh, and we turned and strolled across the street and down a block to King Kamehameha's Crab Shack. Snagging a table on the patio overlooking the bay, we studied the menu, a large chalk board hung above the serving window.

"I think I'll try the crab cakes," I said, mouth watering in anticipation.

"Yeah, those look good," Jed answered, eyeing another patron's plate briefly before looking back to the menu, "but I'm going for the coconut shrimp." He glanced at me, smiled, and said, "You sit still and enjoy the view. I'll go order."

The view was certainly worth savoring. The deep blue waters of Maalaea Bay; the dark outline of hills around the curve of beach; the neat masts of ships in their slips along the dock, as well as the full-bellied sails of those returning from their errands on the ocean's deep water. All covered by a sky so clear and blue it felt unreal. I'd always thought my little corner of Colorado enjoyed clear skies, but that was before I came to Hawaii.

Jed came back carrying plates loaded with delicious smelling food.

"Wow," I said, accepting my lunch. "That was fast."

He nodded, sat down, grabbed a piece of breaded shrimp and dragged it through a deep red sauce. "I didn't expect to be handed our plates as soon as I paid." He popped the shrimp into this mouth, chewed, swallowed, and grabbed another. "This is really good!"

I cut into my first crab cake with my fork, lifted it to my lips and sighed with contentment as the moist, flavorful tidbit hit my tongue. "Oh, yeah," I murmured between bites. "If we were staying on Maui, I could eat here every day."

We finished our meal, but lingered at the crab shack's table, sipping POG, a refreshing passion fruit-orange-guava juice drink, and alternately watching the bay and our fellow tourists. The number of people walking around in skimpy swimsuits and flip-flops made me feel positively overdressed in my khaki shorts and bright pink T-shirt. Of course, Jed and I both wore swimsuits too; we just wore regular clothes over them.

A little after 1:00 we saw the Sea Princess slip into place at Captain Bill's dock. Happy tourists disembarked, their necks slung with cameras, the afternoon sun glinting off sunglasses and binoculars.

Jed stood and held out a hand to me. "Shall we?"

"We shall," I answered with a grin. "I'm really anxious to meet this Maris person. I wonder how Serena expects the girl to help?"

"No clue. I just hope she's actually on the boat with her dad and not off having a picnic with friends or something."

I nodded. We'd made this trip to meet Maris Grainger, and one way or another, we would do so. If she wasn't aboard the Sea Princess, we'd just have to keep an eye on her father, Richard, until he led us to her.

We needn't have worried. When we boarded the Sea Princess, we were greeted by a teenage girl with short, curly red hair, dozens of freckles across her nose ... and a faint other-worldly glow outlining her trim young body. She was dressed much as I was, in neatly pressed khaki shorts and a T-shirt, but her T was emblazoned with Captain Bill's name and logo.

"Welcome aboard the Sea Princess," she said, taking our tickets and checking our names off on a clipboard. "Please find a seat. The mate will explain what we're about in a few minutes."

We walked on. No point it trying to talk to her now; she needed to get the rest of the passengers aboard.

Moving forward, we claimed seats along the bow rail of the little ship. A few minutes later a tall man wearing khaki trousers, a short-sleeved white shirt, and wrap-around sunglasses unhooked a microphone and called for our attention.

"Welcome aboard the Sea Princess," he announced. "I'm Richard Grainger, and I'll be your guide today. We'll be setting sail in a minute or two for Molokini Crater where you'll enjoy some of the best snorkeling in the islands. Our sailing time will be about an hour, so please pay attention while I give you some necessary safety information."

I listened to the man's speech, at least enough to take note of where the life preservers were stowed, but most of my attention was focused on Maris. True, we hadn't asked the teen's name, but normal human girls didn't have a glowing aura.

Frowning, I watched the girl as she moved quietly and confidently across the deck. Something was off. She definitely had a nimbus, but it wasn't as bright and clearly defined as that of most Fae. Hers was somehow softer, more misty than I'd come to expect.

Neither did I see the image of her true form upon her human body. When the Fae choose to be seen by mortal men, they wrap themselves in a glamour. They appear human, no matter what their true forms may be.

Because of our unique heritage, Jed and I see the Fae for what they really are. Our *sight* allows us to see past the image they project to their true selves. We see their human disguise superimposed upon their other-worldly forms.

Maris presented a soft Fae nimbus, but I saw no trace of another form.

"What is she?" I wondered quietly to Jed.

He shook his head and adjusted his sunglasses on his nose.

"I don't know," he answered, just as quietly, "but her father is pure human." He nodded toward our guide. "I wonder if he's really her father, or just some poor schmuck she's ensorcelled into believing they're related?"

"No telling, but we've got an hour to find out what's going on."

Richard Grainger had ended his spiel by inviting the passengers to explore the ship, enjoy non-alcoholic beverages and snacks in the lounge off the galley, and watch for passing humpback whales, which he promised to point out if any were spotted by the crew.

With forty or so passengers moving freely around the decks, we'd be able to approach Maris easily.

"Let me talk to her first," I said, laying a hand on Jed's arm. "We don't want to scare her by ganging up on her."

He nodded. "Okay, but stay in plain sight. We don't know what she's capable of."

I patted his arm. "Don't worry. I won't underestimate her."

Maris stood against the wall in the lounge, presumably keeping an eye on the platters of food in order to restock as needed. I picked up plate, arranged a slice of pineapple, some bits of cheese, and a couple of crackers on it, and then moved to stand beside her while I nibbled.

"This is a nice boat," I said, trying to sound casual. "Is it a yacht?"

The girl smiled and her nimbus glowed a bit brighter. "The Sea Princess is a double-hulled catamaran, a very stable yacht."

I wiped my fingers on a napkin and held out my hand. "I'm Artie," I said, and nodding toward Jed, added, "that's my husband, Jed. We're on our honeymoon." I grinned, blushing slightly.

Maris took my hand. Hers was warm, her handshake firm.

This close, I could see the ghostly image of long, slim fingers, webbed almost to the tips.

"I'm Maris Grainger," she said. "Congratulations."

"Thanks." I released her hand and, picking up a piece of cheese, nibbled a bite. "Grainger," I said, as though considering. "Are you related to the mate who's our guide?"

She dimpled. "He's my dad. We moved out here from Kansas about a year ago."

"Kansas? Really? And you're both working on a sailing ship? That seems a bit odd."

She shrugged. "Dad was a sailor before he met my mom. They lived in Hawaii for a while, but moved inland when I was a baby."

"How interesting!" I glanced around for more people in Captain Bill T's. "Is your mom on board too?"

Her smile disappeared, a deep sadness filling her eyes. "No. Mom died in a car accident in Kansas."

"Oh," I said quickly. "I'm so sorry."

We stood in silence for a few moments. I glanced at Jed, who met my gaze with solemn reassurance. He couldn't hear what Maris and I had said, but stood ready to assist if needed.

I took a deep breath and decided to take the plunge. The lounge held only a few people, no one near enough to hear what I said to her next.

"Maris," I said quietly, "Jed and I, well, we're what's known as *Seers*. We see things other people can't." She stiffened, and I placed a hand on her arm. "We can see that you're not, well, you're not exactly human."

She startled, tried to pull away. I tightened my grip on her arm.

"Please don't leave," I said, putting as much compassion in my voice as I could. "We mean you no harm, but we have a message for you."

She stilled. I knew she was ready to flee, but stood her ground, quietly wary. I dropped my restraining hand.

"What kind of message?"

"Do you mind if Jed joins us?" I asked. "We didn't want to scare you by both approaching you at once."

She glanced in his direction, moved a little to her left, giving herself a clear path to the door, and nodded. "All right. He can come over, and I'll listen, but if you try to hurt me, I'm screaming for Dad."

I beckoned to Jed as I said, "We're not interested in causing you any trouble, Maris. We just need to talk to you."

Jed strode across the room and stopped beside me. "You must be Maris," he said, holding out his hand and giving her his most charming smile. "I'm Jed Kendrick and I'm very glad to meet you.

She put her hand in his, a bit timidly, but managed a smile when he released her after a brief shake.

"I was just about to tell Maris about our encounter last night," I said.

"Great," he said. "Why don't we sit down at that table. We might as well be comfortable while we talk."

Once we were all seated, I told Maris our tale. "We're honeymooning on the north shore of Kauai, and last night while we were strolling along the beach, we met a young woman. Only she wasn't … a woman, I mean. She was a selkie in human form." I paused and studied Maris's face. "Her name is Serena." Maris's eyes widened. She knew Serena.

"Someone stole her skin," I continued, "and she's stranded in human form. She told us about you. Asked us to find you and tell you that she needs help." I paused again, a frown tightening my brow. "The thing is, neither Jed nor I can imagine how you, a teenage girl, can possibly help her."

Maris exhaled the breath she'd been holding and said, "Oh!

That's terrible. I may not be able to help, but I can let her colony know where she is and what's happened to her. They may be able to figure out how to get her home. At least she'll be with her family again, even if she is cut off from the sea."

"Her colony?" I asked blankly.

The girl nodded. "She's a member of a colony of selkies that lives on Ni'ihau."

"The Forbidden Island?" Jed asked.

"That's right," Maris said, nodding. "It's a private island and most of it is uninhabited. It's a haven for Hawaiian Monk seals, and the selkies decided to make it their home as well. They're related to the Monk seals, after all."

"They are?" Jed and I said together.

"Sure. The Hawaiian selkies are descended from a few Scottish selkies who decided to try their luck with human sailing. When their ship was destroyed in a storm, they managed to grab their skins, transform, and swim to safety. They joined a herd of Hawaiian Monk seals and eventually interbred and became the selkies of Ni'ihau."

"Wow," I said. "I had no idea."

"And how do you fit into all of this?" Jed asked. "What exactly are you?"

Maris glanced around the lounge, but we were the only occupants at the moment. The loudspeaker had announced a whale sighting a few moments before and everyone but us had raced to the port rail to see.

"I'm a siren," she said. "Well, technically, I'm only half siren. My dad, as you probably noticed, is completely normal. Evidently my mom was a real siren."

She shrugged. "I'm a little fuzzy on the details 'cause I didn't know anything about it until last year. Mom kept me away from salt water because she didn't know if my blood would be strong enough to allow me to transform, but she knew I'd be drawn to the sea. So I grew up in Kansas."

"And she never told you?" Jed asked, a little callously in my opinion, but then he hadn't been there to see the look in Maris's eyes when she spoke of her mother's death.

"She died before she got around to explaining," Maris said.

Jed had the grace to look uncomfortable. "Sorry," he said quietly.

"But now I know," Maris continued, her tone brightening, "and Dad and I live here now and I get to swim in the ocean with my friends every day."

"So, do you snorkel with the tourists?" I asked.

"No. I stay on the Sea Princess while everyone snorkels." She grinned. "Wouldn't want to scare away the tourists."

"Of course," Jed said with a nod. "You wouldn't need any equipment, and you probably change shape."

She nodded. "Not as much as a selkie, but it's noticeable. I can swim with my dad, but no one else. At least not in salt water. In fresh water, I stay human."

"Fascinating." I said, and Jed nodded his agreement.

Snorkeling at Molokini Crater was wonderful. The turquoise waters were crystal clear, with no sediment to impede our vision. We marveled at the many types of colorful tropical fish as they darted around us, and thrilled to the stately sea turtles that swam so close we could almost touch them. I was truly disappointed when it was time to board the Sea Princess and return to port. But Maris met us with towels and promised to introduce us to a pod of dolphins before we left, so I was content to act the compliant tourist.

As we drove the Jeep back to Kapalua Airport, Jed and I

agreed we'd had a very successful day. We'd done the tourist thing, had a taste of snorkeling in paradise, and had fulfilled our promise to Serena. Best of all, Maris had promised to meet us the next afternoon at Hanalei Bay, where we hoped to give the selkie good news.

It was nice to know that not all Fae were evil creatures. Far from needing to protect humanity from selkies, it seemed that, in Hawaii at least, selkies needed protection from humans!

4
___

The next afternoon we strolled the white sand of Hanalei Bay again, only this time we had to thread our way past beach umbrellas and relaxed people resting on towels soaking up the bright Hawaiian sunshine. Swimsuit clad humans frolicked in the gentle waves, while the more adventurous could be seen adjusting their masks and fins before plunging beneath the surface of the salt water.

Jed and I meandered around the curve of the bay to a rocky outcropping where a lone figure sat staring out to sea, her dark hair billowing in the breeze.

"May we join you?" I asked Serena when we were close enough to speak comfortably above the susurrus of waves and wind.

She glanced up and nodded, a small, sad smile gracing her lovely features. "Of course. It's good to see you again."

I settled on a flattish rock beside her while Jed squatted at my other side. "We found Maris," he said, shading his eyes and glancing out to sea.

Serena sat a little straighter and stared at him, hope shining in her eyes. "What did she say? Will she help?"

I nodded, answering before Jed had the chance. "She said she'd meet us here this afternoon. I don't know when exactly, but..."

"There!" cried Jed, pointing at the water. "I think she's coming. That swimmer is too far out to be a tourist."

Serena and I both gazed in the direction he pointed, and after a moment's searching, I saw something bobbing in the water. Something that came closer and became more distinct as I watched.

"It's her," Serena said, excitement ringing in her voice, "and look! She's not alone. She's brought one of my colony."

A few moments later — faster than I would've thought possible — Maris emerged from the sea, like a red-haired, bikini-clad goddess. She was followed by a seal, who dipped beneath the surface and emerged again as a man with dark hair graying at the temples.

If I hadn't been watching closely, I wouldn't have noticed the unnatural elongation of Maris' hands and feet, or the webbing between her fingers and toes. Her transformation back to human-appearing teen was nearly instantaneous.

The man who followed her onto the rocky outcrop carried what looked like a wet ball of fur, held strategically since he wore no clothes. He didn't seem at all embarrassed by his state of undress. In fact, I had the impression that he held what was undoubtedly his seal skin in that precise location for my benefit alone.

Jed and I rose to our feet as Maris and the selkie approached. Serena jumped to her feet and ran to the man. He dropped his skin and enveloped her in a hug.

"Serena," he said. "We've been so worried. I'm relieved to find you whole and well."

"Father," she said with a sob. "I'm stranded. I can't come home!"

I glanced away from the selkies, feeling that I intruded on their reunion. I turned my attention to Maris instead, and saw that she too carried a wet ball of fur. Puzzled, I glanced back at the father and daughter. No, the man's skin lay at his feet, where he had dropped it to embrace his daughter.

Turning back to Maris, I quirked an eyebrow and nodded to the skin in her hands. But before she could answer my unspoken question, the seal-man cleared his throat.

"The Selkies of Ni'ihau are in your debt, Seers," he said with a formality that rang with Fae magic. The Fae rarely acknowledged obligation to humans, but when they did, it carried a binding geas. Jed reached for my hand, and we held tight to each other.

"We thought our daughter lost forever, but the message you carried has restored her to us." He inclined his head to us, his dark eyes shining with sincerity. "We acknowledge our debt. Word will be sent from dolphin to whale to seal until every one of our kind in the world knows of your deed. If ever you are in need and a selkie is near, we will render what assistance we can." He paused to stare directly into Jed's eyes and then my own. "Selkies do not forget. Never would we have expected such a kindness from a seer. You are unique ... and we will remember."

Chills ran down my spine despite the sun's heat. I knew I should respond, but no words came. My mind felt frozen by the selkie's words.

Fortunately, my husband has always been the socially adept member of our team.

"We acknowledge your gift," he said solemnly, "though we don't feel its need. What we did was a small thing. Carrying your daughter's message cost us little and gained us knowledge, not only of your kind, but of Maris as well. We value such knowledge. Let us part as friends ... with no debt between us."

I squeezed Jed's fingers in appreciation of his words.

The selkie studied us for a long moment. "You are gracious, Seer. We release the obligation of indebtedness in favor of friendship. May the Selkies of Niʻihau and the members of your bloodline remember this day to eternity. Let there be friendship between our people."

He inclined his head to us, and Jed and I responded in kind.

"And now," he said, turning to his daughter, "we must get you home."

Serena sobbed and tears streamed down her cheeks. "But how? My skin is lost!"

Maris stepped forward, speaking for the first time. "Your mother sent you her skin," she said, holding out the dripping fur. "Wear it for your journey home."

Serena's eyes widened as she accepted the skin, stroking it wistfully. "Is this possible, Father?"

He nodded. "Only from a close relative can such a sacrifice be made, and only in extremis, but yes, you may wear your mother's skin for this journey."

He turned back to me and Jed. "We will take our leave now, Seers. Know that our offer of future assistance holds." He held up a hand when Jed started to object. "Not out of debt or obligation, but out of friendship. Farewell, Seers-Who-Are-Friends-of-Selkies. May your lives be rich and fruitful."

"Farewell, Selkies of Niʻihau," Jed responded. "May that which is lost be found."

And with that, Serena and her father slipped into the water, donned their skins, and swam swiftly into the depths of the blue Pacific.

EPILOGUE

*J*ed and I had been home from our Hawaiian honeymoon for less than a month when we received a letter from Maris. I opened it quickly and read aloud.

I just wanted to let you know that Dad and I contacted the police about what was stolen from Serena. Of course, we didn't mention exactly what was taken, only that thieves were preying on tourists on both Kauai and Maui, and that thefts had even happened on our cruises.

The thieves were caught and when the arrest was made, a seal pelt was discovered among the loot. The thieves claimed it was a magical artifact taken from a selkie, but no one believed them. The police saw it as evidence of the slaughter of Hawaiian Monk seals, an endangered species.

Dad says the judge will throw the book at them for that!

Now that Serena's family knows where her lost item is, they'll be able to get it back ... but not until after the trial. The family is anxious for those men to be imprisoned.

Hope everything in Colorado is great!

Your friend,
Maris

I folded the letter and smiled at Jed. "We're friends with a siren."

He nodded. "Not to mention a whole colony of selkies." He grinned and pulled me into his arms. "Who'd've ever guessed we'd be friends with any species of Fae?"

"Certainly not me," I said. "Life is full of surprises."

"Definitely," he said, hugging me even more tightly, "and I can't wait to discover the next one!"

COPYRIGHT

THE JOURNAL

CHAPTER ONE

*A*rtie Woodward-Kendrick pulled down the collapsible staircase to the attic in her childhood home. She'd always hated the attic, had found any and every excuse to avoid going up there. But then, Artie's childhood had been filled with terrors.

Literally.

Creatures no one else could see.

Creatures that fed from the life energy of the people around her. She'd learned to hide from their sight, had learned to keep herself safe. But until she met her husband when they were both teens, she'd had no idea that it was possible to fight them. Her life had changed irrevocably when she met Jed Kendrick, and she'd never been happier.

Time to face yet another of her childhood fears.

Wiping sweaty palms on her well-worn jeans, Artie pushed up the sleeves of her red flannel shirt, grasped the rails of the collapsible stairs and climbed into the dim and dusty attic. She thought she heard something scurry away as she landed on the wooden floorboards, leaving dusty imprints of her sneakers with every step, but her heart was pounding so hard she couldn't be sure.

Where was Jed? He'd agreed to help her with this.

Her parents were selling the house and moving into a condominium and while they sorted and packed the contents of the main floors, she'd been given the task of inspecting the attic and determining what was worth keeping and what should simply be lobbed into the trash bin. She'd wanted to refuse, but her parents were so proud of what they saw as her recovery from her childhood instability ... well, she didn't want to disappoint them. And she *was* strong now. But she was so much stronger with Jed by her side.

She found the slender pull chain that controlled the single light bulb attached to one of the rafters and yanked it on. Light flooded the center of the room, but left the edges and the spaces behind boxes and old wardrobes in shadow. She shivered, but forced herself to walk deeper into the room.

It's just old stuff, she told herself sternly. *There's nothing here that can harm me. It's only creepy because there's not enough light and everything is covered in dust and cobwebs. There's nothing dangerous living in my parents' attic.*

She'd reached the grimy, round window at the far end of the room when a noise on the staircase started her heart pounding again. Turning to face the hole in the floor, she saw a dark head appear. Her racing heartbeat and jittery stomach urged her to scream, but she stifled the impulse. A moment later, she smiled as the man of her dreams stepped into the attic's dim light.

"Hey, sweetheart," Jed said in a cheerful voice as he surveyed the boxes and dilapidated furniture. "Sorry I'm late. How do you want to tackle this?"

Artie released the breath she hadn't realized she'd been holding and gestured around the room. "Pick a box, any box, and evaluate the contents. Let's make three piles: one to keep, one to trash, and one to donate."

"Sounds like a plan," he said, clapping his hands. "Let's get started."

Artie had moved three boxes to the trash heap and one box of out-of-fashion, but serviceable clothes to the donation pile, when Jed gave a low whistle.

"Come take a look at this, Artie."

He stood before an ancient piece of furniture, a secretary her mother would call it. The slanted lid opened to become a flat writing surface and the back portion was filled with little drawers and cubbies for holding who knew what.

"Look what I found," Jed said, his voice loud in the still room. "A kind of secret compartment."

She walked over to stand beside him. What looked like a carved, columnar divider between two of the cubbies was actually a hidden vertical drawer. Jed had accidentally loosened it, and taking a chance, had pulled. It slid out revealing a book with a cracked leather binding and yellowing pages.

But even more unexpected than its hiding place was the book itself. The volume glowed to Artie and Jed's special sight. For Artie Woodward and Jed Kendrick weren't normal humans. They were *Sidhe Seers*. Both were descendants of an ancient Irish clan which had been given the ability to see the Sidhe, the ancient Celtic name for what the mundane world called fairies.

Jed could trace his lineage directly to the ancient O'Connors, but Artie had no idea where her connection originated. She only knew that she could see what she'd always termed *Terrors*, but now knew were a particular race of Fae.

"What do you think it is?" she asked, her earlier nervousness slamming back into action. "Do you think it's safe to touch?"

Jed shrugged. "Only one way to find out," and he pulled the

book from its hiding space, opened the cover, and began to read aloud.

January 30, 1919

My name is Maeve O'Connor Woodward and this is my journal.

I'm a newly married woman and a Sidhe Seer. My husband, Michael Woodward, is an English groom. He accompanied his lord from his home in Somerset to the lord's newly purchased manor in the Dublin countryside last year. Michael and I met when he was sent to my family's farm to buy hay and oats for the lord's stables.

I fell in love with him at first sight. Tall and well-built, with golden hair and gray-blue eyes, so unlike the local lads. I longed to run my fingers through that hair, thick and wavy, it was, and the strands that had come loose from the black ribbon with which he'd tied it back enticed me. His hair didn't spring into unruly curls like my own auburn locks, and I wondered what it would feel like between my fingers. Smooth as silk, I imagined. Not the knotted mess mine so often became.

I'm not sure Michael even noticed me that day, but as I would soon come to know, our fates had been bound by the Sidhe, or as some have come to call them, the Fair Folk. 'Tis my belief that they're so called in order not to offend, for the Sidhe I've seen are far from fair. To be sure, ungifted mortals who've been granted a glimpse of the Sidhe are always astounded by their beauty, but that is because they see only the glamour the Sidhe choose to allow.

I'm a Sidhe Seer, from a long line of seers. I see past their glamours to their true countenances, whether they wish to be seen or not. 'Tis a blessing and a curse. I'm not likely to fall prey to their tricks, but if they realize I see them when they believe themselves hidden … well, 'tis a fine line I walk in order to secure the safety of me and mine.

But I digress.

I was telling you that this is my book. I am keeping this journal

CHAPTER TWO

*J*ed paused in his reading and glanced at Artie. "Well, now we know where your seer blood comes from."

She nodded. "Too bad I didn't find this years ago. It would've spared me a lot of grief to know who and what I am. Do you think we should tell my folks?"

Jed frowned. "You get it from your Dad's bloodline according to Maeve's name ... has he ever shown any sign that he has *The Sight*?"

"No, and he never tried to talk to me, to tell me I wasn't alone." She shrugged. "They both acted like they thought I was nuts and carted me off to a psychiatrist before I learned to hide. I think *The Sight* skipped him."

Jed nodded. "According to Granny O'Toole, that's common." He paused, frowning at the book. "Plus, there's something weird about this book."

"Other than the fact it glows?" she asked.

He grinned. "Yeah, other than that. It's the way she assumes that if you're reading it, you have *The Sight*. I wonder...."

He wiped his dusty fingers on his jeans, grabbed Artie's hand and pulled her to the stairs. "Let's test a theory."

They clambered down the collapsible stairs and wound their way around boxes and packing supplies to the kitchen where Artie's mother, Estelle Woodward, was carefully wrapping dishes in newsprint and wedging them into a cardboard box.

"Hey, Estelle," Jed said, leaning against a counter a few feet from where his mother-in-law worked. "How's it going?"

Estelle looked up at the two young people, wiped a strand of hair out of her face with the back of her hand, and smiled. "Getting there." She leaned against the counter as well, happy to take a break from the repetitive work of reaching, wrapping, and bending. "How's the attic coming along."

"We're making progress," Artie said, finding an open bit of floor space and dropping to sit cross-legged.

"Actually," said Jed, "we just found a hidden compartment in an old secretary. This was stashed inside." He held the book out to Estelle. "Thought you might like to see it."

"How odd," she said, accepting the book and examining the cover. "A hidden compartment ... that sounds very intriguing."

The back door opened before she could say more and Richard Woodward stepped into the kitchen carrying a drill and a small blue tool box. He glanced around in surprise.

"What's this?" Richard asked. "Break time?"

"Jed and Artie discovered a secret compartment in an old piece of furniture in the attic," Estelle explained. She held up the book. "This was inside. Any idea what it is?"

Richard placed the drill and tool box on the counter and took the book from his wife. "No idea," he said, opening the cover and flipping through the pages. "Why would anyone hide a blank book?"

Jed laughed, a bit too heartily to Artie's ears, and took the book back from Richard. "It's a mystery. Probably something someone put away to give as a gift and forgot where they hid it. Interesting old secretary though. Do you want to keep it, or should I mark it for charity?"

Estelle grimaced. "Charity, definitely. If it's been tucked in the attic, we haven't needed it, and we already have too much furniture in the main house for our new condo."

"Right," said Artie, scrambling to her feet. "Well, come on, Jed. It's back to work for us."

"Thanks, kids," said Richard. "We really appreciate your help."

"I'm going to order a pizza for lunch," Estelle said. "We'll call you down when it gets here."

"Sweet!" Jed grabbed Artie's hand and gave her a quick tug. "Race you to the attic."

CHAPTER THREE

Once back in the attic's dim light, Artie turned to her husband. "Well, we learned a couple of things."

Jed nodded. "Your dad's definitely not a seer."

"And Maeve had mad skills," added Artie. "I wonder how she managed to write words that only another seer can read?"

"Dunno. Maybe that'll be one of the lessons she'll cover later in the book." He opened the journal and flipped through the pages, each one crammed with small, precise penmanship. Every page was filled, even the back cover bookplate.

Artie took the book from him, walked to the end of the room and propped it against the grimy round window. "I'm anxious to learn more from my great-great-grandmother," she said, "but right now, we need to earn our pizza."

Jed moved to stand beside her. Placing an arm around her shoulders, he reached out with his free hand and stroked the journal's cover. "We're looking forward to learning what you have to teach, Maeve."

Artie rested her head on his shoulder for a moment, then drilled a finger playfully into his side. "Come on, you. There's sorting to be done!"

As they moved to tackle yet more forgotten boxes, Artie surveyed the attic and sighed with contentment. Yet another childhood fear banished. Too bad she hadn't conquered it years ago. If she'd found that book when she was young, her life might have been very different.

Her gaze fell on Jed, earnestly rifling through a box of long disused household items.

No, she wouldn't waste time worrying about what might have been. The events of her life had led her to Jed, and he was worth every awkward or unpleasant moment she'd ever endured. Knowledge was good, and she didn't doubt that they'd learn a lot from Maeve's journal, but she'd learned from experience that knowledge came when the time was right ... and this book had come to her now.

She smiled and opened another box. Now, when she and Jed could study the journal together.

The timing was perfect!

PALADIN SHIELD

1

My name is Artemis Lucia Woodward-Kendrick. My husband, Jedidiah Amos Woodward-Kendrick, and I recently purchased our first home.

I stared at the words I'd just written in the journal that Jed and I had decided would hold the record of our lives together in this house, our first home.

Our home.

Not my parents' home, or my in-laws, or even Grannie O'Toole's quaint cottage in Dublin. No, this sweet little house on the outskirts of McIntosh, Colorado was *our* home. Jed's and mine. Since we were newly married and as yet unemployed, we'd been able to afford this investment in our future thanks to the generosity of our friend and benefactor, Laird Angus O'Connor.

Life had been a whirlwind since I'd rescued Jed from enthrallment to the fairy queen in Ireland last Halloween. But that horrendous ordeal was behind us now. We were safely married, had enjoyed a fabulous honeymoon in Hawaii— again, thanks to Laird Angus— and had celebrated Christmas with friends and family here in Colorado.

We'd been home from our honeymoon for a scant three months, but already the new year had brought even more change. My parents had decided to downsize, moving from the home I'd grown up in to an upscale condominium on the shore of Lake McIntosh. Of course Jed and I helped with packing and their move, but since we'd been staying with Mom and Dad, that event had also necessitated a search for a home of our own. Jed's parents had offered us a room in their home, but we'd decided it was time to find our own place in the world.

And now, thanks to Laird Angus, we're the proud owners of this lovely little cottage situated on the very edge of national forest land. The cottage sits on an acre and a half of land, shaded by old growth pines and firs. Though it was only mid-March, crocuses and daffodils were already shooting up in the front garden and buds were showing on the apple tree in the backyard.

Inside, the cottage was snug and cozy, reminding me of Jed's grandmother's home in Dublin. The main floor boasted a comfortable living room which Jed and I had furnished with second-hand items, including a few pieces my parents didn't have room for in their new condominium. Like the well-worn brown leather sofa that used to live in the great room of my childhood home and the antique mahogany secretary Jed and I discovered when we were cleaning out the attic.

I smiled, well pleased with the look of the room. From the hardwood floors with their braided rag rugs to the mismatched sofa and overstuffed chairs to the secretary, lovingly cleaned and polished, the room spoke of comfort and contentment. Which was exactly what I wanted.

Opening my *sight*, I studied the room again, this time nodding with satisfaction at the warding runes glimmering on the walls and surrounding the windows and doors. Jed and I would be safe within these walls. No wandering Fae would break through those wards.

Moving into the kitchen, I sighed with happiness. From the cheery yellow walls and white pine cabinets to the farmer's sink, brushed steel appliances, and terra cotta floor tiles, the room suited me perfectly. I glanced across the half-wall with its serving counter to the dining area. Jed and I had found a wonderful pine trestle table and six matching chairs at an estate sale. We intended to share many meals at that table, enjoying the view from the wide windows that overlooked the tame carpet of our back lawn as well as the wild beauty of the old growth forest beyond.

Finally, I turned my attention to the bedroom... and shivered as a tingle of delight ran down my spine. The room was dominated by a king-size rustic aspen log bed topped with an heirloom log cabin quilt done in blues and reds and golds. The quilt was a gift from Jed's parents, but the bed itself was our gift to each other. We'd seen an example of the craftsman's work on a trip to Estes Park and had known instantly we had to have one. The bed was our one splurge. Everything else in our new home might be second-hand, but our bed would be our own. We'd special ordered it that very day, and now here it stood, in our own bedroom, in our own home.

Anticipating the night to come, my heart raced. I was almost as excited as I'd been on our honeymoon! Forcing my thoughts back to the here and now, I continued my examination of the house, moving to the narrow staircase.

Much like Grannie O'Toole's home, our cottage also included a second story—two small bedrooms tucked beneath the eaves with a shared bath. At the moment they both served as storage for the crates and boxes we'd yet to unpack, but we intended to set at least one up as an office.

Of course, an office suggested we had a clue about our future careers. Which neither of us did... at least not yet.

Sighing, I returned to the kitchen. Opening the refrigerator, I removed a pitcher of orange juice, grabbed a tumbler from the cabinet beside the sink, and poured myself a glass. Carrying the orange juice to the trestle table, I sat and sipped the tart liquid while staring at the huge trees beyond the yard and pondering our future. Life had finally settled down. Mom and Dad were happy in their condominium. Jed and I had a place to call our own. It was time to establish a routine, and that meant finding a way to support ourselves. We were adults now. Time to make our own way in the world. No more dependence on either set of parents, or even Laird Angus, the head of Clan O'Connor, and my friend and mentor during those dark days in Ireland.

We needed jobs, but what kind?

Sure, we had skills. Unique skills that had been passed through our bloodlines for generations, but those skills weren't exactly marketable.

Jed and I were hereditary *Sidhe Seers*. We could see what other mortals could not. We saw the Fae— in all their beauty and horror. And more than that, now that we'd found the journal left by my *Seer* ancestress, we were learning that we had the ability to banish the Fae from the mortal world.

But since regular folks had no idea the Fae existed, except in children's tales, our skills weren't exactly a hot commodity. Sure, we'd gone to college. Jed had decent IT skills and I was an excellent researcher, but information technology and library science were unlikely to support us; not when we might have to drop everything on a moment's notice in order to fight an incursion of Fae!

I had no idea how we were going to solve this puzzle, but knew we'd figure it out. I shook my head, remembering what was important: Jed and I were together. When he'd been enthralled by the fairy queen in Ireland, I'd been terrified that he was lost to me forever, that I'd never find a way to rescue him. Yet here we were, married with our own home in Colorado.

Finding jobs would be a snap compared to breaking the fairy queen's hold on my best friend... and the love of my life!

Before I could do more than take another sip of orange juice, I heard the front door open and footsteps pound across the hardwood floor.

"Artie!" Jed's voice called. "Where are you? I've got news!"

2

"*I*'m in the kitchen," I called, placing my glass on the table and standing to meet the man I loved.

Jed burst into the room, strode to my side and swept me into his arms, hugging me tightly. "You'll never guess," he said, twirling in a circle before setting me on my feet and holding me at arms' length.

"What?" I cried, laughing and working to find my balance after his enthusiastic greeting. "What are you so excited about?"

"Angus!" he said, his grin so wide it was a wonder he could speak. "Laird Angus is coming. I just got off the phone with him. He's at the airport now."

"In Dublin? When will his flight land in Denver?"

"No," he said, his eyes alight with merriment. "He called from Denver! He's renting a car and will be here within the hour."

My happy surprise turned to horror. "Here? Now? Jed! We don't have a spare bedroom set up yet." Not that we'd really planned to have a guest bedroom. We intended for those small bedrooms upstairs to be storage and an office. At the moment, both were disaster areas! I glanced toward our bedroom with its beautiful king-size bed and sighed. Our first night in our new bed would have to wait. The laird would have our room and we'd make do with sleeping bags among the boxes upstairs.

Jed laughed and pulled me into his arms. "Don't worry about it, sweetheart. Angus can afford a suite at the Hilton, though I expect he'll make do with a less fancy hotel here in McIntosh."

I sighed, more relieved than I wanted to admit, and nodded. "Okay. Did he say why he was here?" I asked, and then hurried to add, "Not that I'm not delighted, of course, but Colorado is a long way from Ireland."

Jed released me and moved to the cabinet beside the sink. Grabbing a tumbler, he poured himself a glass of orange juice and we settled at the table.

"Not really," he said after chugging half of his juice. "He just said he needed to talk to us and he'd be on his way as soon as he had keys to a car."

I nodded and sipped my juice. I wasn't worried about him getting lost on the way; he'd made the drive from Denver to McIntosh last fall when he'd accompanied Grannie O'Toole to our wedding. But why was he here at all? What could the clan chief of the O'Connors need to talk to us about? I suspected there was more to the man than most people knew— when I first met Laird Angus my *sight* had hinted he was far more powerful, and far older, than he seemed— but I'd kept my suspicions to myself.

Perhaps we were about to discover more about our benefactor.

A little over an hour later, Jed and I stood on our front porch as Laird Angus O'Connor parked a dark blue Subaru Outback in our driveway. I reached for Jed's hand as Angus stepped from the car and made his way to us.

"Mr. and Mrs. Woodward-Kendrick," he said with a gallant bow. "It's pleased I am to see ye in your new home."

"Welcome, Laird Angus," Jed said, letting go of my hand and stepping forward to shake the Laird's. "We're always glad to see you."

Laird Angus turned to me, mischief sparkling in his eyes. "And ye, Artie? Are ye glad to see me?" He cocked his head and raised an eyebrow.

I laughed and threw myself at him, startling him so that I nearly knocked him to the ground, but he caught me in his arms and we hugged each other tightly. "I owe you my life and my happiness, Angus," I whispered, tears gathering in my eyes. "You will *always* be welcome in my home."

Jed cleared his throat and I stepped away from the Laird, wiping my eyes and smiling. "Well, don't just stand there," Jed said. "Come in and see the place you helped us buy!"

Jed and I proudly escorted Laird Angus through our home, even leading him through the mess of the upstairs bedrooms and detailing our plans for them once we'd finished unpacking and could find the floor. We finished by standing on the back deck, pointing out where our land ended and the national forest land began.

"Ah, 'tis a bonny place ye've chosen," he said as Jed opened the patio door and led us into the dining area. "I'm sure ye will be verra happy here." He glanced above the door, his eyes losing their focus, and I knew he was examining our wards. When satisfied, he nodded and smiled at me. "Ye've done verra well. 'Tis proud I am to have ye in my clan."

I grinned. "About that..."

"Aye, yer Grannie Maeve told me. The mystery of yer lineage has been solved," he said, his eyes twinkling. "I'd like to have a peek at that wee journal while I'm here."

"Of course," said Jed, "but before we start talking business, why don't we sit down? Maybe have a cup of coffee or tea?" He cocked his head and continued, "Here or the living room? Your choice, Angus."

The Laird clapped, rubbed his hands together, and nodded. "A cuppa wouldna go amiss," he said with a smile. "Tea, if it's no trouble, and let's settle in that pretty living room."

"No trouble at all," I said, moving around the counter to put the kettle on. "Jed, why don't you show Angus the journal while I make the tea."

Jed nodded and the men left the kitchen.

A few minutes later I carried a tray into the living room to find Angus standing by the window studying the journal Jed and I had discovered in the antique secretary in the attic of the home where I'd grown up; the same secretary that now stood in the corner of this room in all its newly refurbished glory.

"Well," I said, setting the tray laden with mugs of tea and a plate of oatmeal cookies on the oak coffee table, "I'm glad to see you haven't been wasting time."

Angus looked up and grinned. Closing the book he strode across the room and settled in one of the overstuffed chairs. Jed joined me on the sofa and handed out napkins and cookies while I arranged the mugs of tea within everyone's easy reach.

I took a sip of my tea before gazing directly at Angus and asking, "So, Laird Angus, what brings you to Colorado?"

He held up the small book he'd been studying. "This journal for one thing," he said solemnly, and then gestured to me, "and to welcome a long-lost daughter into the clan."

I frowned. "That can't be all. Regardless of that journal, I became part of your clan when I married Jed."

"True enough," he agreed, "but this journal clears up your bloodline. 'Tis good to know which line of my descendants you belong to." He laid the journal on his knee and patted it. "I lost track of this lassie when she came to America. I'm glad to know her line continued and her blood ran true."

Whether he'd intended to or not, Angus had just confirmed my long-held belief that he was far older than he looked. I glanced at Jed and saw with amusement that he'd had no idea. His eyes were fairly popping out of his head and his jaw hung slack.

I took the mug from Jed's hand and placed it on the coffee table, nudging him with my elbow as I did so. "Close your mouth, my love," I said quietly. "You look like he hit you with a two-by-four."

Angus laughed as Jed composed himself. "You're not surprised, Artie?" Angus asked in an amused rumble.

"My insight suggested as much when I first met you in the O'Connor archives," I said.

"But you never said anything!" Jed protested.

I shrugged. "I didn't know for sure. Besides, it wasn't my secret to tell."

"Ye are wise beyond yer years, lass," the Laird said. Turning to Jed, he continued, "I am not only the laird of the O'Connor clan, Jedidiah Amos Kendrick. I am *THE* O'Connor. The first and original *Sidhe Seer*. My longevity is due to the fact that I am half *sidhe*. My father is a *sidhe* prince; my mother was a mortal woman." He shrugged and took a swallow of tea. "And I? I am as you see me... and have been so since before the Romans invaded the British Isles."

"B...but...but," Jed stammered. "But the *sidhe* are FAE!"

Angus nodded. "Indeed they are. *Sidhe* is the old name, the Gaelic name. They've been known as the *fair folk*, which devolved into *fairy*, for centuries now. I prefer to name them *Fae*, myself."

Jed shook his head. "But if you're part Fae, aren't you, aren't *we* hunting your own family?"

Angus nodded. "I despised the way the Fae treated mortals, my mother included, and vowed to protect humans from the *sidhe*." He cocked his head and gazed intently at Jed. "I heard about your interactions with the selkies and that part-siren girl in Hawaii. You didn't banish them. In fact, you helped them."

"They weren't hurting anyone," I said quickly, my cheeks heating and my pulse quickening at the implied criticism.

He held up his hand. "Peace, Artie. I wasn't questioning your decision, merely making a point. If the *sidhe*, the Fae, leave mortals in peace, I'm content to instruct my clan to leave them be. 'Tis only when the Fae prey on mortals that me and mine intervene."

We were all quiet for a few moments, each considering the ramifications of the Laird's remarks. I bit into an oatmeal cookie, savoring the rich flavors of creamed butter and sugar, oats and raisins as I considered the man's long life. Not to mention the fact that I wouldn't exist if he hadn't married in the far distant past and sired children. I wondered exactly how many people alive today could trace their lineage back to Angus O'Connor? Certainly both Jed and I could.

My eyes widened and I inhaled so sharply I almost choked on a bit of cookie. Didn't that mean that Jed and I were related? Should we have married? Would the Laird's revelations end my relationship to the man I loved more than life itself?

My thoughts must have shown on my face, for Angus reached across the coffee table and patted my knee. "Relax, Artie. I checked. Yer line and Jed's parted company before America was even discovered. Ye are nowhere near being closely related, despite the fact that ye both descend from me."

My cheeks heated and I lowered my head, allowing my hair to fall forward, shielding me from his gaze. Before more than a heartbeat or two had passed, Jed touched my arm.

"Don't, Artie," he said quietly. "You're safe with me, and Angus means us no harm. You don't need to hide."

I straightened, pushed my hair behind my ears, and leaned

into Jed's arm. "Thanks," I told him. Turning to Angus, I said, "Forgive me, laird. It's an old instinct."

Angus studied me. "Yer defense is formidable, Artie. I almost lost sight o' ye, and I'm fully aware ye are here." He cocked his head, his eyes narrowing. "I don't think I've ever seen that ability before, though yer grannie did mention she'd seen it once."

Knowing I'd be embarrassed, Jed rubbed his hands together and said, "All right!" before grabbing a cookie, stuffing the whole thing in his mouth and chewing rapidly. He washed it down with a swig of tea, and said, "So, the facts as we know them." He held up a finger. "One: Angus is ancient." A second finger joined the first. "We're all related." His ring finger rose. "If the Fae don't bother us, we don't bother them."

He glanced around. "Is that all there is? You came all the way from Ireland to tell us not to bother any Fae that doesn't threaten us or the community around us? When you already had proof we'd do that anyway?" He narrowed his eyes and pointed at Angus. "I don't think so. I also don't think you came to confess your age. I'm guessing most of the O'Connor clan has no idea you're the original O'Connor. So what really brought you to Colorado?"

Angus smiled and nodded. "Verra astute, Jedidiah. Ye're correct on all counts." He picked up a cookie, took a bite, and chewed. Slowly and deliberately. As if he had all the time in the world. Which, of course, he did. Quite literally.

Jed bounced up and paced around the room, coming to a stop behind the sofa. Resting his hands on the back, he leaned forward and glared at Angus. "Come on, man! Spit it out!"

Angus's eyebrows rose almost to his hairline and he glanced at the last bite of cookie in his hand.

Jed scowled. "Not the cookie," he almost shouted. "The reason for your visit."

Angus finished his cookie, took a swallow of tea, and said, "Oh. That." He glanced at me. "This is verra good tea, Artie."

I tried not to smile as I said, "Thank you, Laird, but I think you need to answer Jed's question before he explodes. He's not as patient as I am."

Jed threw up his hands, muttering in disgust, and strode around the sofa to plop down beside me again.

"Fine," Angus said cheerfully. "If ye must know, I came to offer ye jobs. Both of ye."

3

"What?" Jed and I exclaimed together, though to be fair, Jed almost roared ,while I definitely squeaked.

"Jobs," Angus repeated. "Employment. Ye know, a way to earn money to pay for yer home and food."

"I know what a job is," Jed growled. "I just don't know how you expect to employ us when you're in Ireland and we're in Colorado." His eyes narrowed and he leaned forward. "We're not moving to Ireland, if that's what you're thinking."

Angus leaned back, comfortable in the overstuffed chair. "And why would ye be thinking I want ye in Ireland when 'twas I who ensured ye had the wherewithal to buy this house? Don't be daft, boy. A man who's lived as long as I have has varied business holdings and more capital at his fingertips than ye can imagine." He stopped talking, seemingly engrossed in examining said fingers.

"And?" I prompted before my husband could growl again.

Angus glanced at me and smiled. "I'm opening a Denver branch of one of my IT companies, Paladin Shield. I want the two o' ye on my payroll as consultants."

Jed sat back, his expression neutral. "What kind of IT company and how would we consult?"

"'Tis designed for computer security. Keeping systems up to date and impervious to hacking. I know ye studied information technology at university, Jed, so no one will question yer credentials, but I'm no interested in yer computer skills. I have experts on staff for that. Purely mortal men and women who have no knowledge o' the Fae."

He paused and studied our faces. "Nay, I want the two of ye to be my paladins. My knights— though ye willna be wearing shining armor— to defend humanity from malicious Fae. Ye'll be on the payroll of Paladin Shield, but ye'll have no need to set foot in the building; ye'll report directly to me. The only folk in the Denver office who'll know aught about ye will be the head of HR, who will have employment files that I'll create, and the financial director, who will authorize yer pay."

I frowned. "Why paladins?"

Angus shrugged. "A nod to my longevity. I knew Charlemagne's paladins. Rode with them on a few quests. A more noble group of knights never existed. They were honorable men who fought to protect the people given into their care."

He stopped, his eyes glazed with memories of the distant past. After a moment, he shook himself and met our gazes. "So? What do ye say? Want to become modern day paladins, roaming the earth to protect mortals from dangers they canna even see?"

"Of course," we answered together, then grinned at each other.

"Seriously, Angus," Jed said. "That sounds perfect."

I nodded. "Exactly what I dreamed of, but couldn't figure out how to achieve."

Angus slapped his hands on his knees. "Excellent! Ye'll have access to a private jet hangered at the Denver airport. I'll give ye each a dedicated cell phone just for this purpose and will let ye know where ye need to be when trouble arises."

"Wow," Jed said. "A private jet? Dedicated phones? This is starting to sound like James Bond."

Angus laughed. "Not quite. Ye'll have no 'Q' building fancy weapons and gadgets, but the O'Connor clan does provide me with an enviable intelligence network. Not all of my descendants have the *sight*, but enough do to keep me informed about conditions around the world, and fewer still have the means to fight the Fae. Most can only observe, and that only with great discretion. The two o' ye are unique. Which is why I want ye to be the paladins of the O'Connor clan."

Jed and I nodded, too overwhelmed to speak.

"When you're not on quest," Angus continued, "ye'll live and train here in McIntosh. I'll arrange for a mixed martial arts master to work with ye when ye are in residence." He turned his gaze on Jed. "I'd also like for ye to appeal to yer guardian angel. See if he will join ye in the physical world and train both of ye to fight the supernatural more effectively."

"How did you..." Jed began, then closed his eyes and answered his own question. "Grannie O'Toole."

Angus nodded. "Maeve O'Toole is an invaluable part of my intelligence network. Will ye make the request?"

"I will, but Michael visits when he sees fit, and then only in my dreams."

"I understand," Laird Angus said, "but perhaps a prayer would not be amiss?"

Jed nodded. After all, his father was the pastor of one of the local evangelical churches. "I'll visit my dad's church and pray for intercession."

"Excellent," Angus exclaimed again. He rose and clapped his hands. "Now that our business is concluded, may I take my favorite paladins out for a steak dinner?"

Jed and I agreed readily, and I moved around the coffee table to hug our ancestor, benefactor, and... employer!

4

S pring blossomed into summer before Jed and I were called upon to act as Laird Angus's paladins.

The months between the Laird's visit and our first assignment were busy ones. Angus arranged for a small dojo to be built at the back of our land once Master Kenji approved its placement.

"The trees enfold this space like the arms of the dragon," our sensei told us when we met for our first lesson in our private training space. "You will learn safely here." The sensei worked us hard, meeting with us three days a week and insisting we practice *tai chi* every morning before breakfast.

But mixed martial arts weren't the total extent of our training. We also trained with Michael three days a week. Not the same days, thankfully, but between the sensei and the archangel, Jed and I had only a single day without scheduled training sessions.

True to his word, Jed had gone to his father's church the day after Angus's visit and spent an hour in prayer, asking for Michael's help in defending the human race from malicious Fae. The archangel had replied swiftly. He visited Jed's dreams that very night and listened attentively to Jed's description of the Laird's plan.

"When your training space is complete," the warrior angel had said, "I will come. But you and Artemis will be the only witnesses. I will be invisible to anyone else who happens upon our training."

While Master Kenji taught us to fight, he also taught us to meditate. To clear our minds of all distractions and to act with focused deliberation. We learned calmness in the face of danger, and practiced until our bodies could react without conscious thought.

Archangel Michael also taught us to fight deliberately and without fear, but his teaching concentrated on more arcane methods. From Michael we learned the uses of holy water, of specific prayers for the sanctification of weapons, places, and people. He taught us how to call upon the forces of light and life to aid us in the protection of innocent lives. Michael taught us faith. Not in church or creed, but in the god who created us and the forces of good he had set in motion in our world. Michael agreed wholeheartedly with Laird Angus (and us) that as long as the Fae were not in opposition to that good, they were not to be harmed.

It was an intense three months, but when the call came from Angus in early July, we felt ready.

Jed answered our dedicated phone and engaged the speaker function so neither of us would miss a word.

"And how are ye progressing, my paladins?" Laird Angus asked.

"Michael and Master Kenji are satisfied with our progress," Jed said. "Of course we won't know for sure until we're tested, but I'm confident in our abilities."

"And ye, Artemis?" Angus asked. "Are ye confident as well?"

I nodded, though the Laird couldn't see me. "I am. Jed and I fought well together before our training. We have a lot more techniques to put into action now."

"Verra well," Angus said, and I could almost see him nodding. "'Tis time for my paladins to take the field. Ye are needed in Glasgow. A particularly mean-spirited clan o' Fae have moved into the city. They're terrorizing the citizenry, though the locals are attributing the violence to gang wars and the like."

Jed and I glanced at each other, our expressions grave.

"How do you want us to proceed?" Jed asked.

"Get ye to the airport. I've already alerted the pilot. He'll have the jet fueled up and the flight plan logged by the time ye arrive."

I grabbed a pad of paper and a pen and wrote down the details as Laird Angus fired them off: which hangar to approach; where to park; the pilot's name. All the information we'd need not only for this mission, but for future ones as well.

When all the details had been passed along, Laird Angus said, "One o' my O'Connor lads will meet ye when ye land in Glasgow. He'll take ye to the clan keep. The other *Sidhe Seers* there will fill you in on the specifics. They won't be able to help ye fight, but they'll support ye in any way they can, so don't be afraid to tell them what ye need."

Jed and I nodded. "We understand," I said.

"We'll keep you posted," Jed said.

"Dinna worry about that, lad," Angus said. "The Glasgow clan members will give me regular reports. Ye'll be there to protect the city, not to be doing paper work and chatting with me."

"We won't let you down, sir," Jed said. I nodded my agreement.

"I've every confidence in ye both," the Laird said. A moment later he added, "After all, I've seen young Artie at work first hand."

Jed turned to me and grinned; my cheeks heated with a flush. "She's pretty amazing," he said. "I'm a lucky man."

"That ye are, lad. That ye are."

5

The flight to Glasgow was amazing. I'd never set foot on a private jet before and was overwhelmed by the luxury. Comfortable white leather seats seemed to mold to your body and swiveled for ease of conversation or reclined for relaxation. Deeply cushioned chocolate brown carpeting. Cherry wood tables and architectural accents were polished to a velvety glow. Curved white walls with strategically placed windows for viewing the world as we skimmed above it.

Having only flown commercial flights before, and those only rarely, I was overcome with nerves. I closed my eyes and concentrated on the meditation exercises Master Kenji had taught me. I couldn't afford to allow the butterflies fluttering in my belly to get the best of me. If I gave in to nerves now— over the transportation the Laird had provided!— how would I ever manage to control myself when it came time to battle the Fae?

Jed didn't seem nearly as nervous as I felt. No, my tall, handsome husband acted like a ten-year-old boy turned loose in a candy shop! He sat in every seat but the one I'd chosen, checked out all the cubbyholes, chatted with the pilot, and asked if he could join him in the cockpit and check out the controls. The pilot laughed good naturedly and said not today, but he'd check with the Laird about a future flight.

At last the pilot retreated to the cockpit and Jed settled in the seat across from me. Buckling our seatbelts, we prepared for take-off, which was so smooth as to be practically unnoticeable. The minute we levelled off and the *fasten seat belts* warning clicked off, Jed jumped up and said, "This is awesome! Want a snack?"

I laughed, my nerves dissolving immediately. My Jed was irrepressible!

"Sure. Why not?" I unbuckled my seatbelt and joined him in exploring the compact, but well-stocked galley. We opted for fresh-baked chocolate chip cookies and bottles of spring water. I'd eyed the selection of fresh fruit— apples, oranges, bananas, and a medley of berries— but decided I could be health conscious another day. This first flight was all about luxury!

A little over nine hours after leaving Denver, we landed in Glasgow. While it was only early evening for me and Jed, it was past midnight in Scotland. We disembarked from the jet and were met by a sleepy-eyed man with auburn hair and beard in a rumpled dark blue suit.

"Jed Kendrick and Artemis Woodward?" he asked, stifling a yawn.

We nodded and Jed held out his hand. "It's actually Woodward-Kendrick for both of us," he said, shaking the man's hand. "We decided to combine our surnames when we married."

"O' course," the man said, extending his hand to me. "I'm Gareth O'Connor. Laird Angus asked me ta help ye get settled and act as yer guide." He motioned toward a waiting car. "If ye'll come this way..."

We followed the man across the tarmac, but as he opened the door of the car, I placed a hand on his arm.

"I know it's late here," I said, urgency buzzing beneath my

words, "but I feel a need to confront the Fae now. Before they're alerted to our presence."

Jed nodded. "She's right. It's not even time for dinner yet as far as we're concerned. Take us straight to the area most effected by the Fae's malice."

Gareth studied our faces, his expression revealing his skepticism. Then he shrugged and his face cleared. "Fine. Th' Laird ga' me no specific instructions about yer mission, only that I should gi' ye what aid I could. I ken where th' Fae are most active and if ye wish to go straight there, I'll take ye."

When we were settled in the car and underway, he added, "Ye do understand that I'll no be going wi' ye? If th' Fae know I'm a *Seer*, my usefulness to th' clan will be at an end."

Jed, who sat beside Gareth on what would have been the driver's side if we were in the States, nodded. "We understand."

"We expect to fight alone." I reached forward from the back seat and laid a hand on Gareth's shoulder. "It's what we've been training to do."

"Where are we going?" Jed asked. "And what types of Fae have you seen there?"

We'd left the airport behind and now drove through quiet streets. In the distance, across what I knew must be the River Clyde, lights shone in what was undoubtedly the vibrant heart of the city. But Gareth guided the car away from those lights.

"I'm taking ye to Easterhouse." Gareth's knuckles whitened with the strength of his grip on the steering wheel. "The Fae ha' been riling up those who're disaffected anyway, and the pubs o' th' area ha' been dealin' wi' even more violence than usual lately." He glanced over his shoulder at me. "Two men ha' died in th' last week alone."

Jed and I digested that information as Gareth guided the car across a bridge over the River Clyde. After a few moments, he spoke again.

"As to the type o' Fae, I've seen goblins and redcaps, and..."
— he grimaced and swallowed— "and sluagh."

Jed whistled softly, and I shivered.

Sluagh. The Host of the Unforgiven Dead.

Jed turned in his seat and met my gaze. I nodded, knowing he was thinking as I was that it was a good thing we'd been training with Michael.

"Right," Jed said, directing his words to Gareth. "You'll want to stop a few blocks from where you expect the trouble to be. Artie and I will need to gear up."

We'd entered a part of the city that seemed less well kept. The houses, apartment buildings, and even the businesses had a disillusioned, unkempt air about them. Almost as if the structures themselves despaired of hope and happiness. Gareth pulled the car to the curb and Jed and I stepped out.

My spirit sank as I set foot on the pavement. The very air seemed to urge me to return to the car and escape. I straightened my shoulders and joined Jed as he pawed through the cases we'd brought with us.

"Let's see," he mumbled, almost to himself. "We'll want holy water and the swords Michael blessed." He handed me items as he spoke.

As I buckled on my sword and stowed the holy water in pockets of my calf-length black leather duster, I rehearsed the prayers of sanctification and protection Michael had taught us.

Jed also donned a black leather duster, though he cut a much more impressive figure than my five-foot-two physique could command. Tall and lanky, my warrior husband towered over me. His normally gentle gray eyes flashed with deadly fire as we prepared to battle supernatural forces for the souls of the people of Glasgow.

We moved away from the car as Gareth pointed us in the direction we should go. "I'll shadow ye," he said. When Jed cocked his head and lifted a brow, Gareth shrugged. "I'm ta report on yer success ta th' Laird." He grinned. "And if ye are no successful, I'll be there ta drag yer carcasses out o' danger."

I smiled, but Jed laughed out loud. "Good to know you've got our backs."

Finding the trouble wasn't hard. We heard the ruckus before we turned the corner toward the pub. When we came within sight, we saw a large gang of men slugging it out. Glass from the pub's broken front window glittered in the light spilling from the open door. Men and women stood just inside the door and others leaned carefully over the frame of the shattered window. Those who weren't fighting yelled catcalls, egging their favorite fighters on.

But this wasn't a friendly scuffle between mates. The atmosphere felt dark and malicious. Many of the catcalls were vicious, as if the bystanders thirsted for spilled blood.

I engaged my *sight* and saw the supernatural elements that orchestrated the brawl. Redcaps ensured that falls resulted in cuts from broken glass. Goblins pushed and shoved, making sure no combatants retired from the fight, while the sluagh flitted among the mortals, filling their minds with battle rage and lust for others' pain.

Jed and I glanced at each other, pulled our swords, and strode into the fray reciting prayers for protection of the mortals as we met the supernatural enemy.

Gareth told us later that it looked like a dance—a deadly dance. We slashed and cut, twirled and leapt, separating the Fae from the mortals they sought to harm. The skirts of our dusters flared as we moved from goblin to sluagh to redcap.

Lunge. Thrust. Parry. Feint.

We moved as a unit, always aware of where the other fought as we dodged and blocked, and swept our enemy from the street.

The mortal men and women stepped back as our prayers

took effect. They shook their heads and stared at each other as if wondering why they were bloody and bruised.

But they all turned to watch us fight, and since none could see the enemy, they told themselves they were watching a display of antique skills, for no one fought with blades in this modern world.

When the last redcap fled, Jed and I sheathed our swords amid cheers from the watching crowd. Gareth appeared at our sides, and the barman called everyone inside for a round of drinks... on the house!

―――――――

"They are a sight ta behold, Laird." Gareth spoke into his cell phone while Jed and I packed the last of our belongings. "Th' locals won't be forgettin' the late night *exhibitions* the master swordsmen ha' been puttin' on this seven-day." He paused, listening. "Aye, I'll be tellin' 'em."

Gareth ended the call and turned to us. "He's right pleased, is the Laird. Says ye are ta rest up and be ready for his next call."

Jed and I glanced at each other and grinned. Rest up indeed! Our battles in Glasgow had shown us where our weaknesses were. When we got back to Colorado, we intended to train even harder. We had specific scenarios to describe to both Michael and Master Kenji, and we expected our mentors to help us work out new, more effective strategies.

As he drove us back to the airport, Gareth provided a running commentary on the effects of our work. "Even the locals, those wi' not a whit o' the *sight,* can feel th' change in Easterhouse. Friendlier, they say. There's hope in th' air and folk are cleaning up th' neighborhoods. Men as were fightin' and growlin' at each other a week ago are workin' together ta rebuild and refurbish."

He shook his head. "If I hadna seen it with me own two eyes, I'd ne'er ha' believed it possible." He parked the car near the private jet and helped Jed and I with our luggage.

When we were ready to board, he shook hands with each of us. "'Tis proud I am ta know ye and claim clanship wi' ye. Go wi' grace and know ye'll always ha' friends in Glasgow."

"Thanks," I said, "and the same is true of you. If you ever come to Colorado, we'll be glad of your company."

We boarded the jet, sank gratefully into white leather comfort, and smiled. Happy, but exhausted. We'd survived our first mission. More than survived! We were now full-fledged paladins. Battle-tested and ready to go wherever the clan needed us. We would fight to shield mortals from the wrath and spite of the supernatural enemies they couldn't even see.

Laird Angus had named his IT company well. *Paladin Shield*. We, Jed and I, were the true paladin shield... and we were proud to carry that responsibility. Blessed to be able to protect those given into our care.

COPYRIGHT

ALSO BY DEB LOGAN

Children's Stories and Chapter Books:

Cinnamon Chou Files:

- THE CASE OF THE MISSING INARIAN
- THE CASE OF THE GLITTERING HOARD
- THE CASE OF THE RECREATIONAL THIEF
- THE CASE OF THE VANISHING PUPPY

Prentiss Twins Novels:

- THUNDERBIRD
- COYOTE
- WHITE BUFFALO (COMING SOON!)
- THE TWELVE DAYS OF TRICKSTERS (A PRENTISS TWINS SHORT STORY)

"Read-to-Me" Stories:

- CHATTERMASTER
- DEIRDRE'S DRAGON
- THE FOX AND THE FLEAS
- MOM'S HELPER
- READ-TO-ME STORIES (COLLECTION)

Short Stories:

- ANGELIC VOICES
- LILAH'S GHOST

Young Adult Stories and Novels:

Dani Erickson Stories:

- DEMON DAZE
- SCHOOL DAZE
- FAMILY DAZE
- CHALLENGING DAZE
- DANGEROUS DAZE
- DANI'S DEMONS (COLLECTION)

Faery Chronicles:

- FAERY UNEXPECTED (NOVEL)
- FAERY BEAUTIFUL (SHORT STORY)
- FAERY UNPREDICTABLE (NOVELETTE)
- LEXIE'S CHOICE (SHORT STORY)
- OF DRAGONS AND CENTAURS (SHORT STORY)
- FAERY COLLECTIBLE (COLLECTION)

Feyland Tie-Ins:

- EMMA: A FEYLAND DRYAD
- ON GUARD: A FEYLAND STORY

Seer Chronicles:

- TERRORS
- TO HAVE...AND TO HOLD
- SELKIES IN PARADISE
- THE JOURNAL
- PALADIN SHIELD

Siren Tales:

- Salt Water
- Siren Surf

Short Story Collections:

- Ghosts and Ghoulies
- More Ghosts and Ghoulies

Short Fiction:

- Amelia Fox: Spy in Training
- Beauty or Butterface?
- Rush!
- That Lake House Summer

"WDM Presents" Anthologies:

- Tales of Mystery & Mayhem
- 2016: A Year of Short Fiction
- 2017: A Year of Short Fiction
- WDM Presents: Short Fiction from 2018
- WDM Presents: Short Fiction from 2019
- WDM Presents: Short Fiction from 2020

DANI'S DEMONS PREVIEW

If you enjoyed *The Seer Chronicles*, you may want to read *Dani's Demons*, a collection of tales about Dani Erickson, a teenage demon hunter. Here's a sample chapter.

A shiver of anticipation raced along my spine as Allie and I ducked inside the fortune-teller's tent. My parents didn't approve of psychic nonsense, but they'd allowed me to come to the carnival with Allie's family as a pre-birthday treat. The even bigger treat? Not a single one of my older brothers was tailing me. If the Erickson boys were at the carnival, they were enjoying their own night out, not watching over their baby sister.

Turning fourteen had its advantages!

The inside of the tent lived up to all my expectations. A thick Turkish rug covered the brittle, brown August grass and swags of colorful silk festooned the sidewalls and ceiling, ropes of twinkling LED lights camouflaged within the folds. A small table draped in blood-red velvet sat in the center of the small enclosure. A single intricately carved high-backed chair occupied the far side, while two folding chairs waited for us.

Allie glanced at me as if seeking reassurance. The corners of her lips curved in a timid smile and her eyes widened. "Are you sure we want to do this?"

I grabbed her hand and pulled her to the folding chairs. "This was your idea, remember? We're here. We're not backing out." I plopped onto a chair and waited. Allie lit on the very edge of hers, muscles tensed for flight.

A figure disengaged from the draping silk and approached the carved chair.

"I am Madame Simone. Welcome to my den of enlightenment. This place is hallowed, serving as a threshold to the great beyond."

The olive-skinned woman was swathed from head to toe in a rainbow of silk. Small golden discs dangled from her headdress, gracing her forehead and calling attention to dark, liquid eyes. She studied my best friend for a moment and then turned her attention to me.

"You have come at an auspicious moment," she said, and lowered herself gracefully into the high-backed chair. Leaning forward, she placed long-fingered hands upon the velvet tablecloth. "Tell me what you seek."

Allie uttered a nervous squeak and huddled back in her

chair, moving as far from the fortune-teller as possible without jumping and running.

I glanced at Allie and then faced the psychic. "Aren't you supposed to tell us what we need to know?" I don't like people intimidating my friends.

"What you need to know," the woman murmured, holding my gaze and refusing to allow my escape. "Are you sure you're ready for that? Wouldn't you rather I told you silly tidbits about boys and kisses and who to dance with at homecoming?"

I straightened my shoulders, but didn't look away. Her sarcastic tone bugged me. Allie and I might be young, but we were paying for this woman's time.

"Look, just do your thing, okay? We paid for a reading, so read."

Madame Simone's smile could've frozen Boulder Reservoir. "As you wish." She inclined her head, breaking our eye-lock, and turned to Allie, "Your hand, my dear."

Allie placed her right hand in Madame Simone's left and shuddered slightly when the woman traced the lines in Allie's palm with a perfectly manicured nail.

"I see a long life if you sever your relationship with dangerous friends," the psychic said, spearing me with a pointed glance. "You will dance on the stage to the acclaim of millions. Beware the company of demons."

Allie snatched her hand back the moment Madame Simone released it and cradled it to her chest.

The fortune-teller cocked an eyebrow at me and held out her hand.

Time slowed. My heart thumped wildly, but the air had thickened, making it hard to breathe. Something moved just beyond my peripheral vision, and a desperate desire to flee seized my soul.

And then the moment passed and everything snapped back

to normal. I sat in a stuffy little tent with too many silk drapes and a middle-aged woman who looked at me expectantly.

"Sure. Whatever." I placed my hand in hers ... and a jolt like electricity convinced me I'd made a huge mistake. My hand jerked reflexively, but she held on tight and smiled an enigmatic little grin.

"As I suspected," she murmured, drawing her index finger along my palm and studying the lines like they spelled minuscule words. "You are the seventh ... the child of a seventh ... and you stand at the cusp."

She closed her eyes and held my hand open between both of hers. A sharp intake of breath and her eyes widened and sought mine. Fear glazed her eyes.

"Tomorrow a great burden will descend upon you. Have a care lest it crush you ... and all who care for you."

With that happy thought she released my hand, sprang from her chair and melted back into the shadows.

"That's it?" I yelled after her. "Whatever happened to you're going to meet a tall, dark, handsome stranger?"

Anger mixed with a heavy helping of fear and roiled in my stomach. I wanted to hit someone. Instead, I grabbed Allie's hand and the two of us sprinted from the tent.

"What a load of ..."

"Hush, Dani," Allie said, glancing over her shoulder. "Let's go find my folks."

I huffed, but allowed my pretty little ballerina of a buddy to drag me into the throng of people wandering the midway. Alejandra Chavez had been my best friend since preschool. She was everything I'd ever wanted to be; everything my whole family still hoped I'd become. Dainty, graceful, feminine to the core, Allie was a lady, in all the best senses of the word. She played the piano with finesse and danced like a rose petal on a summer breeze. Of course, grace came more easily to her five-feet-two-inch frame than it did to my towering five-feet-ten-inches. At least, that's how I consoled myself. Whatever my talents were, I'd yet to discover them. I just kind of bobbed along in Allie's wake, never quite measuring up to her shining example.

She pulled to a stop when we spotted her parents tossing rings over bottles at a nearby booth. "Okay. Listen, we don't want to upset Mom and Dad, so let's pretend we never went in that psycho's tent."

I inhaled lungfuls of crisp night air, doing my best to calm my breathing and make my sprinting heart slow to a peaceful crawl. Alarmed parents would only ensure a quick trip home. Besides, there were still plenty of rides and games to explore that didn't involve weird middle-aged women wrapped in silk.

"Gotcha." I nodded. "Everything is peachy. We're having a grand time."

Allie stared at me, a small frown creasing her flawless brow. "Are you alright, Dani? She didn't scare you, did she?"

"Of course not," I scoffed, wishing my stomach agreed. "Tomorrow's my birthday. What kind of great burden hits someone on her fourteenth birthday? I mean, it's not like I'm turning sixteen and Dad's gonna give me a car I could crash. Get real."

Allie smiled a knowing little smile, one that said she saw right through my bravado. She patted my arm and said, "I knew you'd be okay with it. Let's see if we can help Dad win that stuffed tiger for Mom."

I grinned and we joined Mr. and Mrs. Chavez, but I had to force myself not to turn around and study the crowd. Someone was watching us. I could feel their focus ... and my skin tingled in response.

Look for *Dani's Demons* at your favorite online retailer.

ABOUT DEB LOGAN

Deb Logan specializes in tales for the young – and the young at heart! Author of the popular Faery Chronicles series, Deb loves the unknown, whether it's the lure of space or earthbound mythology. She writes about demon hunters, thunderbirds, and everyday life on a space station for tweens, teens, and anyone who enjoys young adult fiction. Her work has been published in multiple volumes of *Fiction River*, as well as in *2017 Young Explorer's Adventure Guide*, *Feyland Tales*, and other popular anthologies.

Sign up for Deb's newsletter and receive a FREE story!

To learn more, visit Deb at:
debloganwrites.com
Or send her an email at:
debloganwrites@gmail.com